LOVE, God, and Mexican Pastries

K.F. Ripley

Love, God, and Mexican Pastries/K.F. Ripley.
—1st ed.
Cover design by Shawnda Craig
Paperback ISBN 978-1-7341731-0-9

Gallina Roja
PUBLISHING

For Brent

Contents

END OF SUMMER

Mom

I plaster my bedroom wall with summer memories. Photo after photo, I tape them up. Lyde and I laughing as he holds up a tiny fish. Bree and I twirling sparklers. The three of us posing all dressed up outside of Bree's church. There are so many, they cover half the wall. And there's still plenty of room for more.

The front door bangs open, slams shut, and her heels come tapping on the floor. I flip through the stack and find a photo Mom will love, one of us cracking up, as her scarf flaps in our faces. I wait for her to throw open my door and say, *Melina, what a great idea!* Outside, the wind starts to blow. I tape up our photo, making sure it's perfectly straight and smooth, and wait. I wait some more. Then I set the stack of photos on my bed, leaving another one of me and Mom on top and go to find her.

An odd stream of light spills out of her bedroom. I push open the half-closed door. In the middle of the bed is a suitcase. Mom walks back and forth, between her closet and the suitcase, piling up blouses, dresses, shoes. She clutches fistfuls of scarves, throws them in, and turns back for more. Mid-stride she stops and presses her fingers to her forehead.

"Mom?"

When she sees me, her whole body sags, like she's carrying much more than a pile of skirts.

"Melina," she says, like she's trying to sound calm, but her gaze darts to the floor and stays at my ankles.

"What's going on?" Her suitcase is piled so high it looks ridiculous. It'll never close.

"I'm sorry," she says, clutching the skirts.

And suddenly I feel something boiling up. I shake and shake and shake my head.

"I can't do this anymore." She holds her hand out like she's presenting evidence to a jury. "Not even for one more day."

But I'm the one in the jury box. And what I see, on the bedside table, is a photo of the three of us at the beach last year, boogie boards in hand, the sun on our shoulders. Best. Time. Ever. "So you're just leaving?"

She nods, barely, but still it's a nod.

"Fine. I don't care," I say. "It's not like we will even miss you." It's a horrible thing to say, and I want to be horrible. I turn around and walk out. I leave her before she can leave me.

Chickens

Cleaning out chicken crap wasn't what I planned when I told Lyde I'd help with his latest do-gooder project. I hadn't really planned on anything. All I cared about was staying away from home. That's my new goal, my I DON'T CARE goal. If Mom and Dad aren't going to care about our family, then I won't either.

Lyde and I and a group from his church are spending the day turning a caged-up chicken farm into a chicken Holiday Inn, complete with a drinking fountain and a wading pool. I swear. I helped haul around the water lines myself.

After the water lines are connected, Lyde and I spend the morning hosing down empty cages, washing chicken turds down a drain. But in the afternoon Mr. Buckley, the chicken farmer, says we've done a good job and promotes us to Chicken Freers.

I set the cage on the ground and open the door. "Come

on, Chicken, let's go." But that chicken just sits there, a giant plop of feathers. "Get out, now. Explore."

"Maybe it's too scared to make the first move," says Lyde.

"You have any chicken feed?" I ask.

Lyde reaches in his pocket and gives me a handful. Then he grabs empty chicken cages in each hand and hauls them out of the pen.

"Here, chicky, chicky." I stoop down a few feet away and hold out the kernels. The chicken looks at me but doesn't move.

I go in closer.

Stare.

I move all the way up and the chicken eats out of my hand. I inch back and the chicken keeps eating and takes one step forward. I move my hand back a few inches. Another step. And then another. When the chicken steps out of the cage into freedom, I scatter the feed on the ground and the chicken starts peck, pecking up all the kernels and strutting around, exploring. She flaps those wings like she's dancing. Another chicken runs over, and in a flash they're having a giant, flapping dance party.

Lyde hauls in two more caged chickens.

"You know that's going to be me soon?" I nod at the happy chickens.

He puts down the cages. "You mean at the harvest dance? You'll go with me and shake your tail feathers?" He grins.

I laugh and give him a shove like I always do, because he's messing with me like he always does. "I mean I'm getting out of this town. Won't be long and I'll be gone."

Just like those chickens, soon I'll be strutting around PSU—Portland State University. I'll have my own dorm room, in a place filled with people. And all day long we'll be calling to each other saying: *Hey, let's go grab lunch* or *When's that paper due?* or *Do you have notes from psych class?* And in the morning, the halls will be filled with the sound of showers running and at night the smell of pizza delivery. And when it's time for class, there will be thundering down the stairs. And brand new everything, new notebooks and binders and books, with pages so crisp you have to be careful you don't get a paper cut. And new thoughts and ideas and theorems.

I won't ever think it's too quiet. And I won't sit around waiting to hear the click of her key in the lock, and mostly, most of all, I won't miss the song of her coming in the door and calling out, "Melina, hey! How was your day?"

Bree

I have Lyde stop me by Bree's house straight from the chicken farm. I'll hang out, then go to my regular Saturday job, cleaning the offices at my dad's work.

"So… I'll see you tonight?" asks Lyde, as I get out of the car.

"Really, you don't have to," I say, even though I'd love his help.

"I can at least help you vacuum, after you helped with all those chickens."

"Yep, you totally owe me," I say, grinning, knowing that if there were any kind of good-deed scorekeeping, Lyde's numbers would be astronomical, while mine would hover in the single digits.

I walk up the sidewalk, ring the doorbell, and try to wave Lyde off, but he's waiting to make sure Bree's home. *Come on. Come on. Be home.* I tried texting but she didn't answer. Probably misplaced her phone again. From inside the house, I hear:

"Got it!"

"It's my turn!"

Bree's brothers slam around against the door. When it opens, there they are with red faces and messy hair. "Melina!" shouts Gordo, who's kept his baby nickname but lost his baby fat.

Fernando smiles and smooths his hair down.

"I wanted to get it." Gordo slugs Fernando in the shoulder, but the older brother doesn't flinch. Gordo grabs me and pulls me into the hall. "I got new Legos." Quickly, he drops my hand. "What's that smell?"

Fernando steps back and covers his nose. "Uh, did you step in dog poop?"

"Sorry, I was helping some chickens."

"Pee-ew," says Gordo, plugging his nose.

"Well, those chickens stink," says Fernando.

"Melina smells *mal!*" shouts Gordo, and they run off, punching and kicking each other down the hall.

"Mel!" In a swoosh of bouncing hair and bracelets, Bree comes rushing in.

"Hey, *amiga mía,*" I say, flashing her a please-have-pity smile.

Quickly, she covers her nose with her hand. "*Híjole!* What land of sick did you come from?"

"Sorry," I say, biting my lip. "Today was that thing at the chicken farm."

"You smell like you should be set on fire." She tightens her hand on her nose and nods. "Follow me," she says, walking down the hall and into the garage. "Take those clothes off and you can shower here. I've been wanting to try something new with your hair anyway. And hurry, if *la madre* smells you in here like that she'll have an attack of *los nervios.*"

Hiding behind their van, I strip down and wrap myself in a towel Bree brought out. Back inside, she pushes me into the bathroom. "Here—use this. And this. And this." She hands me bottle after bottle of body scrub, shampoo, and shower gel. "And if that doesn't get the stink off, I'll run down to the fire station and get the powder they use for dead bodies."

I pucker my lips. "*Besa mi culo,*" I say, and shut the bathroom door. She's always trying to teach me Spanish and *kiss my butt* is one phrase I never forget.

Bree, short for Abriana Josefina Consuela Rosario, and I have been friends ever since seventh-grade Spanish class with Mr. Diaz. He assigned us a paper, but she convinced him to let us do a skit instead. Wearing an eyeliner mustache, I strummed a couple of chords on the guitar and together we sang the *Ay, ay, ay, ay, canta y no llores* song. We laughed so hard we had to start three different times. But we finally pulled it together and both ended up with A's on the assignment.

Showered and dried, I check my phone.

MOM: *Melina, will you call me? I'd love to talk.*

Turns out, I don't want to talk. I press *delete.*

LYDE: *hey i forgot. next month the church group is doing adopt a highway. U in?*

No more chicken turds?

nope. just nice sanitary road clean up

Oooo I can't hardly wait

I'll save you a safety vest.

I do look good in florescent yellow

No call from Dad. No text. Nothing. Has he even noticed I've been gone all day? I help myself to Bree's closet, pulling on jeans and one of her not-too-frilly shirts. "Where'd you get this?"

"I think my mom bought it."

Of course. I look around the room. The pink, ruffled bedspread, the movie-star vanity, a closet full of clothes. Bree's mom is that type. The kind who takes Bree shopping on Saturday afternoons or plans special girls-only trips. Not my mom. She was the type to make sure I turned in all my homework. The type to say: *you're smarter than that*, the time I got an A minus. And now, I guess she's the type to pack up and move out.

School

Lockers clang all around me. Everyone rushes out. I'm the only one who wants to stay, who wishes I could find a place to study all night. I swing up my backpack. It's so heavy I have to lean to the side to carry it.

The custodian pushes around a giant garbage bin. A couple of girls hang up a poster. In one classroom, some lucky guy is still there, staring down at a paper on his desk. I'm halfway down the hall when it hits me… the dark hair… broad shoulders… Quick as anything, I back up and peek into the classroom.

"Marcus?"

He looks up. "Oh hey, Einstein girl."

I smile, a big one, one that feels like a hundred-watter. He remembers the nickname from years ago. "What are you doing here?"

"Me? Going to school. It's the law, you know." He grins and looks at me with eyes like blue Jolly Rancher candies.

Marcus wasn't in school most of last year, but he looks the same, maybe taller, more solid.

"Really, it's good to see you," I say. I've known Marcus since eighth grade when we had physical science together. He sat behind me and would let out a low whistle whenever he saw my test scores.

And then there was the time at the end-of-the-year party, at the Roller-Rina, right after Micky Espelin was goofing off, when he tried to make a sliding stop but crashed into me, making us both fall to the ground, and after that, Micky yelled, loud enough for the whole school to hear— *Geez Melina, keep your giant water-ski feet out of the way.* Right after that, while everyone was still snickering, Marcus came over and asked me to skate the next couple's song.

Marcus leans back in his desk. "Good to see you, too, Melina."

"Where've you been?"

He shrugs. "Here and there, around, you know."

But I don't know. It was the big gossip last year. Marcus was the star pitcher on the baseball team, and right before the season started he disappeared, just vanished into thin air and no one heard from him.

"But you're back for good now?" I ask.

He nods. "Yep, start tomorrow. Maybe we'll have a class together."

I nod and wish it were true, but it's almost impossible now. Every one of my classes is advanced placement. "What are you working on?"

He shrugs. "It's for math class. I guess they're trying to figure out where I belong."

I step closer. Marcus's test is mostly blank. He puts his pencil on the first question. "Maybe you could help me with this one," he says, his eyebrows shooting up.

I laugh. "Don't they want to see what *you* know?"

He taps his pencil end on his chin and grins wider. "You haven't changed: still smart as ever."

"Dude!" says one of the guys, and like turbo-charged bulldozers, Frank and Tyrell plow into the classroom. Frank grabs a desk by Marcus and sits on the top, while Tyrell grabs a chair and plops himself down. Freshman year and sophomore year, the three guys were inseparable, going from one sport to another: football, basketball, baseball. Last year Frank and Tyrell did hockey, too. Frank sat across from me in US History and kept bragging about a big game where he'd gotten his tooth knocked out.

"School's over," says Frank.

"Let's go hit a bucket of balls," says Tyrell.

Suddenly I get that fish-out-of-water feeling. Three guys, all big and sporty, and me, who's most comfortable with books and papers and pens.

Marcus flashes those eyes at me. "What about you, Melina? You want to go hit some balls with us?"

I blink at the invitation. My only sport is running and I've just started that recently. "I'm not really that into baseball."

He grins. "A bucket of *golf* balls."

"Oh sure," I say, feeling my neck heat. "Sure. Yeah, golf. If you mean golf, then I could totally go golfing," I say like I'm Tiger Woods. Why? Why did I say that? I don't know one blasted thing about golfing!

Just then, in comes Ms. Jhaveri. "Well, Mr. Townsend, your math placement isn't supposed to be a team effort. Everyone out. Now." She motions with her arm like she's a tour guide.

"Hold on, guys. I'll hurry and finish," says Marcus, as he frowns at the test.

Frank checks his phone. "I've got work in an hour."

"Yeah, I better roll," says Tyrell.

Ms. Jhaveri taps Marcus's test with her finger. "Let's focus on the job at hand."

"Okay, yeah. See you later," I say, tucking a strand of hair behind my ear. I walk out, wishing something would make Ms. Jhaveri disappear.

Piano

The next day at school I scan the crowd for Marcus, the way you do numbers in a lottery ticket. First period, nothing. Second period, nothing. It's like he disappeared again. Then third period, I spot him outside the chemistry classroom right as I'm going in. He's surrounded by the usual guys, Frank and Tyrell, plus René and Kensly, two girls on the soccer team. I wonder if this is a sports thing, if they're so used to being in a team, they can't split up, even if they're going to be late for class.

"Hey," I say, trying to catch Marcus' eye. I'm about to blurt out, *how about that golf?* But just as I get close, Kensly grabs his arm and pulls him over, whispering something to him. And I pass right by without him even knowing.

I stay at the public library until it's closing time and they kick me out. It's not the best—no fridge, no cupboard with pretzels and chips, and the librarian with the red lipstick gave me the tsk-tsk finger when she caught me unwrapping a granola bar—but it's better than home, where I keep jumping at every sound, hoping it's her coming back.

When I go home, Dad's on the couch hunched over his laptop reading the news. "There's leftover pizza in the fridge," he says.

"Okay," I say, knowing he means frozen pizza, not the good kind like Round Table's. That's all we've had since Mom left—frozen pizza, frozen lasagna, even frozen hamburgers. Before, Dad used to cook and most nights we'd sit down and eat together. But now I microwave a slice of thin cardboard pizza and take it straight to my room.

I prop up my broken-down laptop with a pillow. The hinges are worn, about to give out, and the letter F on the keyboard only works if I push it twice. Next year, for sure, I'll need something new to take to the university. Maybe if I get a scholarship big enough, it will cover a new laptop. I click around and open my folder with practice SAT questions.

Out in the living room, Dad starts playing the piano. Sometimes, if Mom wasn't too busy, they'd do that together. She'd start humming a tune and he'd plunk around finding the melody. Then pretty soon they'd be there together, sitting tight on that bench. Mom singing and Dad along for the ride. I scroll down and down my screen, passing the easy math section and going onto the reading part.

Dad pounds those keys. He's thundering out every note, but it's not that kind of a song. It's an old Simon and Garfunkel song, a love ballad, but he plays it like he's chopping wood.

The thick paragraph of words starts to blur. Dad keeps punching out each note, each chord, he goes up the keys, crescendoing to the final notes… and then *slam, slam, slam*, he hits that last chord three times.

I wait, trying to catch my breath, even though all I've been doing is listening.

Something crashes and bangs and it's not the piano keys. I run into the living room. Dad's off the piano, he's pushing and shoving one side of it. The piano bench has tipped over on its side with all the music spilled out.

"Dad?"

He's shoving and shoving, his face turning red.

"Dad!" I shout. "What are you doing?"

The wheels creak. The old upright piano moves forward. The light on top of the piano falls, crashing to the floor.

"Wait!" I yell.

He shoves harder and harder, pushing that piano

Under the wheels, a scratch appears on the wood floor.

"Dad, you're scratching the floor!" I yell, but it's like he's in a trance. "Can't you wait?"

He doesn't stop.

I run over. There's a penny stuck under one of the wheels. "Just stop! One second."

He pauses, shaking out his arms, and I scoop the penny away. Then he's back at it, shoving until his veins bulge. The piano plows forward, pushing up against the rug, making it bunch up.

I grab the corner of the big oval rug, folding it over on itself and then move the dining room chair out of the way.

"Where are we going with this?"

"Outside," he says. He grunts and shoves harder.

I can tell there's no arguing with him, so I grab the other side and start to pull.

Preacher

The preacher's voice moves up and down like waves. "God knows you. And loves you. Every single one of you. You are a child of God."

I shift on the cold metal seat at the Wednesday night youth meeting. Next to me, Lyde nods like he believes every word. Bree stares straight ahead like she believes, too, even though her church is different, more formal, with giant ceilings and her brothers strapped into ties.

Around me, a couple of guys are on their phones and a girl writes something on her wrist. They look like me: bored, ready to be done with this preaching part, ready for the *super fun games* Lyde said we'd be playing. But I wonder if they're secretly listening.

I haven't been to church in a long time. Dad took me a few times when I was little. At first, the preacher seemed nice, but by the end of the sermons he was always red-faced and sputtering, going on about hell and damnation. He looked like an angry bird, flapping his arms in that robe like he was trying to flap his way to heaven.

On a small stage up front, there's a guitar and sparkly blue drum set. I nudge Lyde. "What about the music?"

"That's for Sundays," he whispers.

Lyde asked me to come to his youth group before, bunches of times, for movie nights, softball, food bank collections. Finally, tonight I said yes. Better here than home; better anywhere than home.

"God loves you with an infinite love," says the preacher. He paces in front of us wearing jeans and a button-down shirt. He turns pages in a Bible. "John the Beloved teaches: 'He who does not love does not know God, for God is love.'"

God.

Love.

The preacher tosses out those words like life preservers, ones I could swim to and hold on. He stops pacing until he stands across from me. "Tonight, I want you to know that God offers you his love."

I stop squirming.

"And God's love is forever."

Forever? What does that even mean? Mom packed up forever. She put it right in the middle of her suitcase. Then she lifted forever up and carried it away.

"I won't be here to supervise."

"There are security issues."

"I don't want to be responsible."

I ask my teachers one by one, until finally, Ms. Newel, the brand-spanking-new teacher, says: yes, she'd be happy to let me use her classroom after school. She says she'll be in and out, anyway, with all her prep work, so I might as well make use of the classroom.

I scoot two desks together and set my books, notebooks, and binder on top of one. On the third, I set out a can of pop and a bag of pretzels. Sure, it's not exactly right, not the same as home, having Mom look over my shoulder and say, "Nice work there." Or "I like what you did here." But at least I can snack and study. I flip open my binder and I'm making a homework checklist when I hear the squeak of someone's shoes.

"Dang, Einstein girl." Marcus stands in the doorway. "Now I know why you're so smart; you never leave school."

"Of course I leave," I say, grinning. "I have to go out for food sometimes." I point with the eraser end of my pencil. "What's that on your shirt? Are those eagle wings?"

"No, Air Force." He stands up straighter. "Fly, fight, win: that's their motto. As soon as school's over, I'm enlisting."

"Nice." I nod. "Me too."

"You… in the Air Force?" He blows out a breath. "That's going to be some heavy competition."

I laugh. "No, I mean I'm leaving town too, PSU— Portland State University, to study biology."

"Phew," he says, wiping imaginary sweat from his forehead. "That'll give me better chances of getting in."

I smile and shake my head while he turns to go.

Marcus flips back around. "You know, I started school a week late and I'm doing some catch-up. Can you look over a math problem and help me out?" He swings off his backpack, which looks as heavy as mine, but he shrugs it off like it weighs nothing.

I squish my books out of the way, making room. He slides right in next to me and pulls out a notebook. He smells like outside, like grass and wind and trees.

The math problems aren't hard, some graphing of relations and functions. I show him the first one, and he catches on quick and starts plowing through problem after problem.

I shuffle through my own assignments and start on some chemistry.

"What about this one?" Marcus sticks the end of his pencil on a long problem with three different parts to solve. It looks fun; a challenge. I dive right in, sketching out a graph, multiplying and dividing and equalizing both parts of the equation. When I'm done, I set down the pencil with a final click.

Marcus blinks. His face looks blank.

"Sorry." I bite my lip. "Did I go too fast?"

"That was nuts. It's like you were in a trance or something."

I shrug. "It's just the way I do it."

"Well that, Melina girl, was amazing."

His words echo around and around in my head, and then they settle in, like they've found the perfect spot.

El Mercado

The three amigos—Lyde, Bree, and I—drive out on the old highway, passing empty fields. On each side, as far as you can see, there's nothing but sagebrush, sand, and tumbleweeds. We keep going for a couple of miles until finally there's a little one-pump gas station and, next to that, a small pink building. Above the arched doorway, in big swirly letters, it says *El Mercado*.

Bells jingle as Lyde opens the door and we walk inside. The smell of Mexican pastries greets us and I stop and breathe it in.

"*¿Qué tal?*" calls a man from the back.

"*Bien*," says Bree, as we shuffle inside.

Lyde and Bree head straight to the bakery, and I walk the aisles. Every row is filled with bright-colored labels: greens, reds, yellows, and blues. Cellophane-wrapped candies hang in long rows. There are boxes and bottles, juices and jellies, beans and vegetables, rows and rows of things I've never tried, never even seen before.

When I get back to the bakery, I grab a silver tray and tongs, but the bin with the sweet bread is empty.

"You'll have to ask the baker," says Bree with a grin.

"Will you do it?"

"*Qué va,*" says Bree

"Come on," I try, pleading, but Bree's lips look superglued shut.

"Lyde?"

"You've got this, Mel."

"And you call yourselves *amigos,*" I say shaking my head. I step up to the counter. "*Hola,*" I say, to the man who's kneading a big blob of dough. His apron is splattered with flour and he's wearing a Dodger's baseball cap.

I point to the back, to the tray of pink-frosted *conchas.* "*Por favor…* um." I feel like a fool, but now that I've started I push through. "Um… *dos… conchas.*" He grabs a paper bag and puts two in: one for now, one for later when I'm studying. But if Marcus is with me… "Oh no, no," I say. The baker looks confused. "I mean…"

"*Yo quería…*" corrects Bree.

"*Yo quería…*" Quickly I count in my head. "*…cuatro, por favor.*"

"*Cuatro pasteles,*" he says. He slides two more in the bag, folds the top and hands it over.

"*Gracias*," I say.

"Nice!" says Lyde.

"See," says Bree. "I knew you could do it." She practically bounces as we go over to the checkout counter. "I am such a great teacher."

"Humble, too," says Lyde with a grin.

Bree looks at my bag. "So, are the extras for your dad?"

"Are things… better?" asks Lyde. He stares at me like he's trying to read my mind.

But this isn't the time. I don't want them to look at me with their eyes full of *I'm so sorry* and *Geez, that must be rough.* I can't tell them how Dad still walks around in a daze, how he barely seems to notice me, and now how he's moved the piano outside and plays it out there like some crazy person. "No. They're for someone else."

"Someone else?" Bree's eyebrows shoot up.

I shrug. "Just this guy."

They both look at me, like they're ready to bring out handcuffs and interrogate me.

"A guy?" repeats Bree.

"We just studying together."

"What guy?" asks Lyde.

"It's Marcus."

"That guy on the baseball team?" asks Bree.

"Didn't he disappear last year?" asks Lyde.

"No. I mean… yes. I mean… sure, he's on the baseball

team and yeah, he disappeared for a while but it's all no big deal. He's just a guy who needs some help with math."

"What happened? Did he get sucked into the Bermuda triangle? Go into witness protection?" asks Lyde.

"He didn't say," I say.

"It's suspicious," says Lyde.

"It's exciting," says Bree.

"Really, guys, it's nothing. No big deal."

Sand Dunes

I help Marcus study two days that week. Chemistry, math, biology—he needs help on all of it. He still doesn't tell me what happened last year, only that he didn't study much and he has a lot to catch up. On Friday, when we finish the last of his homework, he mentions the sand dunes. He says he's helping Frank bring the firewood, and a big group is going to meet out there. And if I wanted to, I should go too.

Sand. Our whole town is built on sand—shifting, moving, changing sand. We do have a river that runs through the middle of town, the giant Columbia River, big enough for boat races every year, but everything else is sagebrush, desert, and sand. We even sing about it in our school fight song: "You're the best in the land, for we know you have sand, Pasco High, rah, rah!"

Uncle Charlie teases me about it when he comes to visit from Portland. *How's my desert rat*, he says. Once, as a joke,

I filled his trunk full of tumbleweeds and he mailed me back an umbrella. When I'm gone, I won't miss the sand. And it won't be long now. The stars are lining up, starting to mark out the path.

Bree has play practice, but I convince Lyde to go with me to the sand dunes. On our way out, we stop at 7-Eleven. I press the lid on my drink and check my hair in the reflection on the pop machine. The other night, Bree said I should wear more eyeliner. She said that without it I look as plain as a piece of toast. "What do you think?" I ask, turning to Lyde. "Do I look like a piece of toast?"

Lyde's straw squeaks as he sticks it into his lid. He sips and studies me. "Toast? Definitely not toast. With your freckles, you look more like banana bread," he says, grinning.

I check my reflection again.

"Come on, Mel. You look as great as a striped bass."

"A fish? Really?"

"I love fish. Now come on. Let's go."

When we get to the dunes, Lyde tucks a bag of marshmallows and some roasting sticks under his arm, and we start hiking. Sand seeps into my sneakers, the wind whips at us, but I keep going, climbing toward the glow of the bonfire.

As we get closer, I squint, looking for Marcus. The air is hazy with smoke. One group sits around the fire. Another group tosses a Frisbee. A few couples walk together. Frank tosses some wood on the fire and when he sees us, he comes jogging over. "Did you bring food?"

"Yep," says Lyde, holding out the bag. "You want some?"

"Dude," says Frank, as he grabs some marshmallows. He calls out, "Hey, there's food over here." And in a flash, Lyde is swarmed, everyone laughing and grabbing marshmallows and rushing back to the fire.

"I'll roast you one," says Lyde, as he goes with the group.

"Maybe later." I walk off a little. A couple of speakers belt out music. Some people dance. Others just stand around. With the sand blowing, it's hard to see. So far, no Marcus. Did he really want me to come tonight or was it just something to say because I was helping him with his homework?

I circle around the fire, going slow, checking each shadowy person. If Marcus isn't here, maybe I'll just sit for a while with Lyde. I won't go home until it's late. Until I'm so tired, I fall straight asleep without lying there in the dark first, wishing to hear the swashy sound of Mom brushing her teeth.

I'm about to go back and roast a marshmallow, but then, a little way down the dune, I spot a shadow I haven't seen before. My heart starts to drumroll but I whisper, *no big deal* and walk over. "Hey."

The shadow turns around. It's him! But across from

31

Marcus is Kensly, her blond hair held back by her signature headband. She looks like Goldilocks, but they say she plays soccer like Godzilla, stomping around and biting everyone's heads off if they mess up.

"What?" she says, like I've just stepped into her goalie box.

"Hey there, Melina," says Marcus. A sudden gust pelts us with tiny sand granules, stinging my eyes and making my mouth as dry as a hundred deserts. Kensly crosses her arms.

"Um… keys. I'm just looking for some lost keys? Have you seen any keys?" They both glance around at the miles and miles of sand dunes and then back at me like I just arrived from looney town. "Well, sure. Let me know if you find any," I say and then I take off, walking fast.

Fine. Whatever. There's my answer. Marcus really didn't want to hang out with me. It was just something to say, like *how are you* or *have a nice day*. He didn't really mean it. I jog away, pounding at the sand with each footstep. And when I'm far enough away that no one can see me—I flat out run. Pounding each footstep into the sand. I run because that's what I do now. A few months ago, when Mom and Dad started fighting, I started running. I push harder, my legs strong and lean. The wind flows along with me. Up one dune and down the other. The sand doesn't slow me down. I'm too strong for that. I run until my breath escapes out in great big puffs.

Finally, I stop, sit down in the sand, and wrap my arms around myself. I look out at that giant sky and I wonder if there's some far-off place out there, a land of no disappointments. A land where moms stick around. A land where, when guys say, *hey, see you at the bonfire*, they really mean it.

I sit in the sand for a good long time and then finally get up and brush myself off. Maybe now I'll have Lyde roast me a marshmallow. As I get closer to the glow of the bonfire, I stop again to stare up at the sky.

"So, you're a star-watcher too?"

I jump.

"Sorry, I didn't mean to scare you," says Marcus.

"I wasn't scared," I say. "I was just… practicing my jumping."

"Well, nice jumping," he says, but even in the dark, I can see him smile.

I start walking away. "Well, I should go."

"Already?"

"Yeah, maybe Lyde wants to go or something."

"Don't leave yet."

"Why not?"

"Because… I mean… I was hoping to see you without all the books and pencils and stuff."

I nod over to where he was before. "Aren't you here with Kensly?"

"Kensly? No. I mean… we're friends and everything. But she's, I don't know, kind of young."

"Isn't she our same age?"

"She's a junior and you know, she's different. All she thinks about is soccer and high school stuff. She doesn't have big goals she's working for like us."

And with that word, *us*, I feel like I'm part of something special. Us. We. Marcus and me.

"Hey, look at that," he says, pointing at the stars. He points up, but I look down, because now, he's holding onto my elbow. His warm fingers press softly into my skin. The sand starts to feel wobbly and heat rushes from my elbow all the way through my body. Marcus is saying something about a flashing light. But I can't concentrate. All I can feel is his hand holding me.

"It's the last Delta connection."

"Connection," I repeat, nodding. I look to where he points. Way off in the distance a couple of white lights soar through the sky. "Oh, you mean the plane." Of course, he meant the plane.

"Most likely it's from Seattle or Portland. The last flight of the night."

I watch as the plane makes its own way in the night.

Way too soon, it starts to descend and Marcus lowers his hand.

"You know, that'll be me up there someday," he says.

I nod. "You mean when we leave this town?"

"No, I mean flying the plane. Maybe someday I'll fly a plane like that, but first for the Air Force."

"Oh, that's right." He's so close I can smell his spearmint gum.

A girl yells. Then there's more yelling and whooping. A group of shadows comes running and yelling and speeding right towards us. They run close, kicking up the sand.

"Come on, Melina, we're dune diving," says Lyde as he runs by.

"You game, Air Force?" I ask.

"What about you, Einstein girl?" he says.

We take off running. It's Kensly who gets to the top of the highest dune first. Marcus and I catch up. She backs up several steps, sprints to the edge, jumps, and disappears. We peer over and watch her tumble down the dune. Arms pulled in, hair flinging across the sand, headband still in. People come from behind, jumping and then spinning, rolling down the dune and turning into shadows. Marcus is so close I can feel the heat from his body.

"Ready?" he asks.

I take one look at Marcus and jump.

FALL

Studying

I love the way Marcus taps the eraser end of his pencil on his forehead, like he's knocking on the door of his brain, trying to get the answer. And his handwriting fits him, with tall L's and the S's that curve around like airplanes flying tricks.

"So how did you get so smart, Einstein girl?"

I feel my face getting warm. "I'm not that smart."

"Come on," he says, laughing. "You were in the gifted group in elementary school, the scholars in junior high, and now you're probably top of the class."

I pick up an empty Reese's Peanut Butter Cup wrapper off the desk and move my finger along the package, flattening the front. Top of the class? It's either me or Anton, depending on who has the most AP classes. "Really, it's nothing; lots of people get good grades."

Marcus shakes his pencil. "Not lots, and most of them you can't even have a conversation with. Take Anton—he doesn't ever open his mouth unless he's correcting your grammar or telling you that you screwed up a decimal point. You, Melina girl, are the whole package."

I'm sure the blush has taken over now and my neck is covered in red splotches, but I can't help it, I smile big and bold.

Wednesday Youth Group

At first, Mom would text every couple of days, but now she's up to once a day.

Melina, it's been much too long. We really need to talk.

Melina, I know this is hard. If we can keep communication open, we'll work this out.

Melina, please, won't you call me?

But my answer is always the same. *Delete. Delete. Delete.*

The jeans-wearing preacher comes over and sticks out his hand. "Hello, Melina," he says. "Marvelous to see you again."

"Oh, sure." I shake his hand and look away. It's my third time here, but I don't want the preacher to think I'm a regular. That I'll be here every week, sitting in the front row and shouting *amen* every time he opens his mouth. It's just better here than home, that's all.

The preacher moves on, shaking more hands. Lyde is

complimenting a girl on her new braces, and when he's done, I pull him aside. "What's tonight's activity? Did you say something about pumpkin carving?"

"That's next week."

"It's not chickens again, is it?"

"No," he says with a grin.

"Okay… okay… thank you all for coming," says the preacher. He waits until everyone's quiet. "Today, we will be putting scripture into action. 'If ye have done it unto the least of these, ye have done it unto me.' We will be helping Jesus Christ by caring for those around us."

He breaks us into groups. He assigns one group to visit old people in an assisted care center, another group to mow and weed the lawns of some sick people. "You three," says the preacher pointing to me, Lyde, and a guy with long hair and a black concert T-shirt, "can deliver food items we've collected to the food bank." As the other groups shuffle out the front doors, Lyde leads us to the back.

"So pretty much we're free physical labor?" I tease.

"Better than spraying off chicken poop," he says.

"True, very true."

Lyde motions to the guy next to us. "Mel, this is James."

"Hey," I say. James smiles and nods, his hair falling into his eyes. I'm not sure what else to say. Something like… *Well, what do you know? It's not even Sunday, and here we are at church.* But that seems too weird so I just stay quiet.

Down the hall, pushed up against the walls are boxes and bags filled to overflowing. Peanut butter, canned pineapple, tuna, soup, mandarin oranges, pancake mix. We load everything up in the back of Lyde's truck and then squish inside. I shove fast-food wrappers and Big-Gulp cups under the seat and slide over, making room for James. Before Lyde even starts the car, James plugs his phone into the aux cord. "Dude, you have to listen to this guitar solo."

In a second, Lyde and James are both head bobbing, fingers moving, faking like they're playing that solo themselves.

"The guitar? Really? You were always the drummer," I say.

"I'm a man of surprises," said Lyde.

"He's a natural," says James. We drive through town that way, with me stuck, squished in the middle, and the two guys air-guitaring on the sides. When the drum solo comes on, I take over. "If you've moved onto guitar, I'll take over the drums," I say. I pound and thrum my air-drumsticks as fast as possible.

All too soon, our fake jam session is over. We get to the food bank, unload and restock the metal shelves, arranging the food in separate areas, just like at the grocery store. The whole time a lady wearing a thick, plastic apron keeps thanking us over and over. "Please tell your pastor how much this means. These supplies come in the nick of time."

We finish a little later than we were supposed to. When we get to the church, the other groups are already seated, looking at the stage. We slip into three empty seats and the preacher starts. "Many of you carry heavy burdens. From Psalms we read, 'Cast your burdens on the Lord and he will sustain you.'"

A guitar is still propped up there in the corner of the stage, unused. "Does the preacher play the guitar?" I ask.

"Shh," says Lyde, but then he whispers, "There's a group that plays on Sundays."

The preacher paces. "Have faith. Trust in God. Believe and He will make all your wounds whole." He walks right in front of us and stares at me, like those words are custom-made for me.

Faith… trust… believe, sure those are nice words, and the preacher seems nice. But what does that even mean? Am I supposed to have faith that Mom will show up on the doorstep someday? That Dad will want to barbecue chicken for all of us? That we'll all sit around laughing and playing Uno again? Am I supposed to have faith in that? Is God something to count on or something to make a wish on? Like blowing a ball of dandelion fluff in the air.

Tardy

On my way to physics class, I see Marcus yanking books and notebooks out of his locker until he's got a huge stack in his arms. As I get closer, I can hear the jet line of swears he's muttering under his breath.

"What's going on?" I ask.

He shoves the pile back into his locker in disgust. "That massive chemistry packet, the one we worked on all last week, I can't find it and I'm supposed to turn it in—right now."

"It's not here?" I check his locker. Not turning that in could drop him one or even two letter grades.

He takes out his binder and flips through it. "Mr. Bowers is a total jerk. He refuses to give credit for late work."

"It's not that he's a jerk," I say, holding tight to my books.

Marcus gives me a look.

"He's like… a tough coach. He wants us to prepare for what's coming… for college… for jobs. He's just intense."

"Well, his intensity is going to kill my GPA and screw my chances with the Air Force."

The halls are emptying. I should go. I take a step back. "I've got to take a quiz," I say.

But the way Marcus stands: jaw tight, shoulders slumped, shaking his head. He looks so alone. So mad. So defeated. It's the same way I've been feeling the last two months, so I can't just walk away.

"Bowers hates me," he says.

"Why? He's a good teacher."

"Maybe if you're a straight-A student. But not me. He has it in for me." Marcus crams the binder back into his locker. "I don't know why." The corner of his mouth twitches up. "Okay, I might know why."

"Wait," I say, grabbing Marcus's arm. "That wasn't you, was it?" Everyone heard about it. Someone in class tossed a match into the garbage bin, starting a fire. It wasn't huge, just a small one. But when Mr. Bowers saw the smoke, he ran over and tried to stomp it out. He got his shoe stuck in the metal wastebasket and ran out of the classroom, clang-stomping around until, finally, another teacher held the wastebasket and Mr. Bowers yanked his foot out.

Marcus holds up his hands. "All I did was give Frank the candy wrappers. I didn't know what he was going to do. He lit the match. It wasn't my idea and I still got stuck with a week's worth of detention."

"Really, Marcus. You've got to pick better friends."

"There is this smart girl I'm hanging out with now," he says with a grin.

"Well, that's an improvement." I grin right back at him.

The second bell rings, and the few students in the hall take off.

"That's it. It's too late. I'm sunk." He throws the binder back in his locker and slams it shut. "I bet I left it at home."

"Maybe I can miss one quiz." I say. "How far away is your house?"

"Ten minutes."

"Come on. Let's go get that packet." I start jogging down the hall.

"What about Bowers?" says Marcus, as he joins me.

"I'll talk to Bowers. Sophomore year I ran his study hall. If I tell him I've been helping you, he'll accept your packet for sure."

"You and your smart-girl magic," he says.

We get to the stairwell, and I feel so light and strong, I leap the stairs, taking them two at a time.

"Can you drive?" asks Marcus.

"Sure," I say, as we rush into my car. "Too many speeding tickets?" I click on my seatbelt and put the car into reverse.

47

"I have a couple," he says. "The Air Force doesn't like it, and if I want to fly commercial someday, the big airlines don't like speeding tickets either."

"They're that strict?"

"I've got to become a responsible citizen and all that crap."

Marcus directs me north of town. After passing a few streets with houses, we turn onto an old highway, zooming out into the country, passing alfalfa fields and apple orchards until we get to his farm. "Turn here," he says.

We drive a gravel road toward a two-story brick house with white shutters. It's lined with plants and flowers and stretched out in front is a deep emerald-green lawn that looks like it was just mowed. "That's my grandparents' place," says Marcus. "Ours is around back."

The road changes to dirt, bordered by tall wispy grass. We bump along until we come to a small house with a faded yellow door. Three slanting wood steps lead up to the door and there's a yard gnome on each of them. I park and a floppy-eared dog comes barking and running from behind the house. "I'll grab that packet," says Marcus.

My throat is dry as sand, and I'm curious. I still don't know why Marcus disappeared last year. Maybe his house holds some clues. "Can I get a glass of water?"

"You want to come inside?"

"Yeah?"

48

He shifts in his seat. "I'm not sure if that's a good idea."

"We've got time," I say, checking my phone. "And I drink really fast."

"It's not that. It's…," He looks out the window. "My mom."

"Okay?"

"She's a lot. You know." He pushes at his forehead like he's trying to push out a headache. "Well, she… talks a lot."

"At least she's around to talk to," I say, surprised at how fast words tumble out.

Marcus blinks, like he's about to ask something but the dog's barking has reached high velocity. He jumps up and down outside the passenger window, like he's ready to break in if we don't hurry. Marcus laughs and says, "Whatever, let's go."

He opens the door, and the dog jumps on his lap. "Hey there, Champ." He rubs the dog's head and ears. Out of the car, Marcus grabs a beat-up tennis ball and hurls it. The dog sprints away.

"I didn't know you had a dog."

"The only good thing about farm life." He rushes up the porch steps and I follow.

Inside, there's a floral couch and loveseat and on the coffee table, a plastic bin filled with nail polish. Not just reds and pinks, but every shade, the names printed on the top: Luscious Lemon, Electric Blue, Metallic Gold.

Marcus goes into the kitchen. It's separated from the living room by a breakfast bar. There's his chemistry homework on top of a pile of mail. "Stupid… so stupid to leave it here," he mumbles. He goes over to the sink, fills up a glass of water, and comes back. "You know, our old place was tons better. It was big, right on the river with a swimming pool."

"I think this is nice," I say, as he hands me the glass.

"It's nothing like our old house."

"Marcus!" In walks a lady with big, silver-dyed hair and lime-green nails that match her billowy sundress. "You're home! And you brought company!" she says, clapping her hand once.

"We're not staying," he says, his face turning cloudy. "We've got to get back to school."

"Nonsense. Why don't I make you a snack?"

"Really, Mom. I've got to get back to class."

She flits her hand in the air. "It's your senior year. Live a little."

"Grades are important," says Marcus.

She turns to me. "Always studying. Always so serious. Tell me, you're not like that, are you? You've got to let your hair down and relax at times. Don't you think?"

"Mom, this is Melina," says Marcus.

I smile, not knowing what to say. His mom seems a little different, but she's here, even offering to make us food.

Champ barks at the back door. "Does that dog have water and food? I won't be responsible for that dog," says his mom.

"I filled his bowl this morning."

"Maybe you forgot."

"Agh!" says Marcus. He pushes the chemistry packet into my hand. "Hold this." He rushes into the kitchen and out the back door.

His mom comes over, a little too close. "You like Marcus, don't you?"

Suddenly, it's warm in here. "We're friends." I use the packet to fan myself. "You know, study buddies."

She raises an eyebrow. "Of course you like Marcus, everyone does."

"Just friends," I say, trying to sound casual. "Like Harry Potter and Hermione." I take a few steps back. But she sticks close.

"We can work together. We've got to get Marcus to forget about joining the Air Force." She leans in. Her breath smells like potato chips. "Why does he want to take off and leave me alone? Why doesn't he want to take over the farm from his grandpa? There's rarely anything life-threatening about farm work. The most dangerous thing around here is the tractor, and tractor injuries are rare. If they happen, they usually only take off a finger or two, not your whole

51

arm or leg or worse. I mean, why would he want to go out and get himself killed?"

The screen door slams behind Marcus. "Let's go, Melina."

"Nice to meet you," I say on our way out.

She follows, pats my arm, and smiles. "We're going to get along just fine." She turns to Marcus. "Don't stay out too long."

"Mom! It's school! I have to get to school," he says, as we hurry down the steps.

She follows. "Some things are more important than school."

"And some aren't," he says under his breath.

I crank the engine and hope she's at least a kind of right. Because I probably just flunked my first quiz.

Zips

Outside, Dad's wearing his blue striped pajamas, playing the piano on the carport. Tonight, his playing seems to be following the weather. He starts with a soft, floating melody, but as the wind picks up and begins to howl, his music turns into thundering runs and heart-breaking chords.

It's so loud I can't believe Mrs. Woodbury hasn't come over to complain. With the wind blowing Dad's hair in crazy directions and his pajamas flapping so violently, I decide to go against my "I Don't Care" goal. I push open the glass door and call out, "I'm making some scrambled eggs. Do you want to come inside?"

He doesn't look up. His hands don't leave the keys. He just shakes and shakes his head.

Marcus shuts his textbook. "That's it. Melina Abrums, you cannot make me study even one minute more."

I look up from the essay I'm writing, fine to be done. After all, it is Friday and we've been studying hard all week. But still, I feel like I should at least act hardcore. "Quitting, already? I thought you were tougher than that, Air Force."

"You know, even prisoners get food, water, and bathroom breaks." Marcus picks up an empty pretzel bag, mashes it, and shoots it into the air. It sails in a perfect arc right into the garbage bin.

"Okay, okay." I laugh and pile my books. We stuff our backpacks, hoist them up, and make our way through the school and out to the parking lot. Being with Marcus all afternoon, him smiling at me with those eyes and calling me *Einstein girl.* Us sitting so close that sometimes our arms touch. It's felt so different than the suffocating quiet of home, I don't want it to end. "So… big plans for tonight?"

"Before anything, I've got to get some food."

"Where's your favorite place?"

"The one with the shortest drive-thru line."

I shake my head. "You're kidding right? You wouldn't just eat at anyplace."

He grins. "Okay, smart girl, where do you go? Who has the best burgers in town?"

In a flash, I'm there. The yellow vinyl booth, crinkle fries, and tiny cups of dipping sauce. Dad telling us about trying to sell a football-themed house with Astroturf for carpeting, a goalpost entertainment center and even a brown-football shaped toilet. Mom laughing so hard, she had to fan herself with a napkin.

"Zips," I say. "Hands down, the best burgers in town."

"All right." He grabs my backpack strap and leads me over to his car. "You've talked me into it. Let's go to Zips."

We find an empty booth in the back of the restaurant and slide in. Marcus's tray is piled high. Besides his double-bacon burger, the girl behind the counter loaded him up with a massive order of fries and extra dipping sauce. When he slipped a dollar bill into her tip jar, she flipped her hair, smiled, and practically sang—*thanks so much!*

Even now, with Marcus sitting across from me, the girl keeps looking over like she's hoping I'll magically disappear and she can run over and slide into my seat.

"That girl's staring at you." I nod toward the counter.

He turns around. "Oh, that's Stefania."

"An old girlfriend?" I ask, teasing.

He shrugs. "It was a long time ago."

"Oh," I say and quickly look down at my fries, wondering if the number of his previous girlfriends is as overflowing as the fries on his tray.

"You know I got a ninety-two on my chemistry test. Ninety-two! I swear Bowers thinks I cheated." As Marcus leans up, his knee bumps against mine. He doesn't move it away but keeps it there like our knees are kissing.

"You'll probably do even better next time."

"Maybe next time I'll get a hundred and Bowers will be so shocked, he'll start growing hair on that bald head of his."

We finish our food and go out to the car. Marcus takes off, driving real slow. Because he's scared of getting a speeding ticket or because he doesn't want to go home yet either?

"Thanks for the burger," I say.

Marcus shrugs. "I ate all your pretzels."

"And my Reese's Peanut Butter Cups," I add, teasing.

"True." He laughs. "You know, if we're going to be spending all this time together you should probably know something about me."

"You mean, the reason you disappeared half-way through the school year?"

"Nah," he shakes his head. "Not that. This is something kind of vital. Something really important. I need to tell you…" He eases the car slowly around a corner. "About…" He fiddles with the air vent. "Well… about my addiction."

Addiction? Is that why he was gone last year? Did he go into drug rehab or something? I hadn't heard any rumors. But maybe I've been too busy studying.

"Yeah." He scratches his nose. "It's part of this addicts-anonymous program I'm in. I need to let people know."

I try to check his eyes, but he's focused on the road. His eyes don't seem bloodshot. His hands don't shake. Do I even know what signs to look for?

The stoplight ahead turns yellow. Even though he could've made it, he brakes and brings the car to a stop. "It's a special kind of addiction."

I scoot a little closer to the door.

"I don't like to tell just anyone. Only the people that I'm closest to."

"Okay," I say, with the tiniest shake in my voice.

"It's not your every day kind of addiction. It's something different." He looks over at me.

I nod, even though all the cells inside me are running around screaming like their hair is on fire.

"I'm addicted to…" he flashes me a grin, "peanut butter." Those candy blue eyes laugh at me. "It's been that way ever since I was a kid. I used to hide jars of it under my bed. Your Reeses will never be safe around me."

I reach over and shove him, but he's so solid he doesn't move.

"Hey," he says, faking like he's hurt, rubbing his shoulder.

"Seriously, you're a dork. A giant colossal dork."

On Wednesday, after studying, we get Blizzards at Dairy

57

Queen. Then on Friday, we go out to the movies. Pretty soon, we fall into a routine. Mondays, Wednesdays, and Fridays, we study and then hang out.

With a mom who ran off to Seattle and a dad in a piano-playing daze, Marcus becomes my life preserver, the one person I can hold onto.

Theater

Opening night at Bree's youth production of *Fiddler on the Roof*, I wait on the sidelines, searching for Marcus. The volunteer ushers are pushing candy sales, shoving programs into hands, and hurrying everyone to their seats. When a guy comes out wearing big headphones and shouting "places," I step out the main doors and into the dark. The parking lot is quiet and still. No cars come screeching in to park. No one comes running up the stairs.

I drum my fingers against the rail. Maybe Marcus is late because of farm work. Maybe a sprinkler pipe broke, or he had to watch a fire. Farmers burn off weeds in the fields, don't they? Maybe a fire got out of control and he had to put it out.

Loud applause seeps through the closed door. The wind picks up. I cross my arms and rub my hands up and down my goosebumps. The red shirt I'm wearing is thin and not my style, but it makes Bree happy. Every opening night, me, Lyde, and the whole Rosario family wear red. That way, when Bree scans the audience, she knows everyone in the red line is rooting for her.

Inside the theater a violin starts to play.

"Melina?" someone calls.

I squint in the dark. I know that voice. It's not Marcus. Dad comes rushing up the stairs and gives my shoulder a squeeze. "Hey kiddo."

"What are you doing here?" I peer around him in the dark, wondering if Marcus is close behind. "Have you seen Marcus?"

They'd met a couple of times. Once when Marcus and I had finished studying and neither of us had any money, we went to my house and ate frozen burritos. And another time when I accidentally took his binder home, and he stopped by to pick it up.

"No…"

My phone buzzes with a text from Marcus.

hey! sorry some stuff came up. I can't make it. C u later.

Yesterday, when we were working on quadratic equations, he didn't say anything about *stuff*. He's supposed to be with me tonight. And later, after the play, all of us—Me, Marcus, Bree, and Lyde—we were supposed to hang out. Bree and Lyde keep bugging me. Saying I'm so busy tutoring him, I don't have time for them anymore.

"Well, I guess he's not coming."

"Then, I guess I get you to myself," says Dad, smiling.

I roll Marcus's ticket in my hand. I want to tear it into tiny pieces, but I just roll it up. Fine. Whatever.

Dad looks down at the ticket. "Won't I need that?"

"It's okay. They don't take tickets after it starts." I stuff the ticket in my pocket. Dad opens the door, and we go find our seats, hunched over in the dark.

Of course, Bree is fabulous. We practiced so many times, I mouth the lines as she acts them out. She has this way of making the mom character so solid, so stable and real.

After the play, after the standing ovation and congratulating Bree and the cast, Bree and Lyde try to get me to hang out with them, but I shrug them off, using the, *too much homework* excuse.

At home, I go straight to the freezer and pull out a tub of ice cream. Dad fills the kettle, turns on the stove, and sits on a barstool. One of the kitchen lights keeps flickering like it can't decide whether to stay on or off. The ice cream is frozen solid, and I try to muscle through but only get a sliver.

Dad stares. "Can I give you a hand?"

"I've got it." I tighten my grip and chisel at the glacier.

"Melina, we need to talk."

Slam! I pound the scoop. I just want ice cream. I don't

want to talk. And I sure don't want to remember how Bree and Lyde looked at me when they saw that Marcus didn't show.

"About this Marcus fellow. Are you dating him?"

"No. I'm fine. It's fine," I say to the chocolate pieces.

"A relationship should be about give and take, about harmony."

Harmony? Really? What happened to his harmony? She's a four-hour drive away.

"Maybe you and Marcus are playing different songs."

I set the scoop down with a clang. "We're not playing songs. We're not doing anything; we're just friends."

"You spend so much time with him. I hardly see you anymore." He takes off his glasses and rubs his eyes.

I chomp down on the inside of my mouth so I don't yell, so I don't say, *I'm not here because I hate it here. I hate our family without her here.*

"And what about your grades?"

"My grades are fine. I told you. I'm doing just fine." The kettle starts bubbling and squeaking.

"Your last semester grades were low. I've never seen them like that, and today I got two separate emails from your teachers. They said they're worried about you. You're missing assignments, failing quizzes, and you've even skipped class."

"Dad, really, I'm working at it." I press hard against the

counter top. Okay, I had a couple of B minuses last term, but I can easily get them up.

"I won't stand by and watch you invest all your time and effort into someone who will just walk away."

I turn to face him. "Dad, this isn't about you. It's about me. And Marcus isn't going to walk away."

"For your own good, I don't want you seeing Marcus until your grades are back up. I'm sorry but—you're grounded."

I take a literal step back, as if I've been slapped. Which, in a way, I have. "But you can't!"

"I'm sorry. I mean it. I don't want you with that boy until your grades are up."

I walk out of the room as the teakettle screams.

Muddy Boots

The next morning, first thing, Marcus is standing by my locker. Why now, when he didn't show last night? I go straight to my locker and start on my combination.

"Hey, Melina," he says, looking up from his phone.

I spin and spin the dial. "What are you doing here?"

He slips his phone into his back pocket and leans against the wall. "I'm really sorry about last night."

Sorry? So was I. Sorry I'd stood around waiting for him. I yank the latch and open the door. "You missed out. It was a great play."

"Last night was a mess. I had to bale alfalfa. It's supposed to rain today, and if it gets wet, it's ruined."

"Why didn't you say anything about the farm work before?" My binder falls to the floor and papers fly all over. Marcus bends down and helps. He's wearing farm boots, muddy, scuffed-up ones.

"My grandpa insisted I stay at the last minute. The

whole night was rotten. Anything would've been better than getting yelled at for not driving the tractor straight." He hands over a pile of papers.

"Thanks."

Frank and Tyrell come over, shoving and pushing each other around, like Bree's little brothers. "There's the no-show," says Tyrell.

"Our ex-friend," says Frank.

"I've been busy," says Marcus.

"Since when are you too busy for lifting?" asks Tyrell.

"School work, farm stuff. I'm busy," says Marcus.

"Uh, huh," says Frank. He looks at me all wrinkle-lipped, like I'm to blame.

"Well, stop being so busy," says Tyrell. He and Frank, throw some fake punches at Marcus and then take off, joining the basketball players strutting down the hall.

"See," says Marcus. "I'm messing up with everyone."

I guess I can't be too mad if he's choosing me over his guy friends. "It's fine. No biggie." I shut my locker and he follows me to class.

"Also, I need to ask you something."

"I'm pretty busy," I say, figuring he's got a paper or a test coming up. I'm behind in all my classes. Homework, quizzes, tests, I've got tons to work on.

"It's about the dance." He nods at the giant poster

hanging in the hall. "I was wondering if you wanted to go with me?"

The dance? I look up at the poster. Harvest Dance is written in giant pumpkin letters. I've always secretly wanted to go but no one's ever asked. It's a big deal, fundraiser for the FFA, dress-up dance with a live band, great food, and held at the Big Red Barn outside of town. I shake my head, not believing he just asked me.

He pushes a dark strand of hair away from his eyes. "Oh, sorry. You probably already have a date."

"No. No date yet." Bree always has a date. But no one thinks of asking me, the study queen.

"Well, then, you should go with me."

All the little cells inside me start running around, fist bumping and body slamming each other. "Sure. The dance. It'll be fun," I say, trying for my most casual.

"Great then." He squeezes my arm. "See you later."

I walk down the hall, grinning as big as the giant harvest moon painted on the poster. But then right in the middle of my over-the-top happiness, I remember—I'm grounded.

Stubborn

When Marcus shows up in Ms. Newel's classroom to study, I don't mention that I'm grounded from seeing him. Dad's whole *you're grounded* thing is about me getting my school work done. If I'm doing homework, that's the most important thing. I can't help it if Marcus sits down next to me and studies too.

I can get around the studying part, but it's the dance part I can't figure out.

I wait a couple of days, hoping Dad will relax and change his mind. When he comes home from work, I'm the picture of a perfect studying daughter, at the kitchen table staring hard at my biology textbook. He opens the fridge and asks, "What should we do for dinner?"

"Anything."

"Well, I can whip up something more delicious than *anything*." He pulls out zucchini and carrots.

I tap my pencil on my notebook. "So, Dad, there's this big dance coming up."

He sets down the vegetables. "You need to concentrate on school work."

"I've been studying all day."

"I checked online. You're missing several assignments in physics."

"I know. I know."

He pulls out the chopping block and a knife. "I've been too distracted." His eyes seem droopy. He looks around, like maybe he's noticing the things that aren't there. Mom's purse on the counter. Her glass of Diet Coke. Her coat hanging over the chair.

All my muscles go tense. Just because she's gone, he doesn't have to act like her, all strict and serious. "All I'm asking for is one dance. A few hours."

"Melina." He sets down the knife. "Your grades are important, now more than ever."

"I told you already. I'm working on it."

"My final answer is no."

I slam my books together, grab them up, and go to my room.

I'm forced to put my I Don't Care goal on hold and talk to Mom. She's been texting and wanting to talk. Mom used to

68

be the strict one and Dad the soft. But now, maybe they've both changed. Maybe when she hears about Dad and his unjust verdict, she'll say he's being ridiculous. Maybe she'll run straight into some Seattle boutique, find me the perfect country dress, fly home, and set Dad straight. Maybe this is the kind of faith the preacher was talking about.

I tap my feet, trying to shake out my nervous energy as I wait for her to pick up the phone.

I wait.

This is Annette Abrums with Braxton, Hensly, and Chidister. Sorry I missed your call. You can also try me at our Seattle branch office, at 844…

I hang up. I won't call her stupid office in stupid Seattle. A couple hours later, I try her phone again, but still— no answer. It's not until late when she calls me.

"Melina! I'm sorry. I wanted to call you earlier, but I've been in depositions all day long. I didn't even take a lunch break."

"It's okay." I swallow down what I really want to say, something like, I didn't really expect you to call back anyway.

"I've been missing you. You should come for a visit. The leaves are changing—vibrant golds and crimsons. Fall in Seattle is breathtaking."

"Don't you hate all the rain?"

"You get used to it."

"And how it's always cloudy?"

"The sun comes out sometimes, too."

"Hum," I say. I pick my glass up off the counter. There's a ring of water left. "There's this dance coming up." With my finger, I trace an M in the water. "And Dad is being really stubborn."

"Well…"

"He's refusing to let me go to this dance with this guy."

"Okay…"

This is where she's supposed to stick up for me. Tell me how unfair Dad is being. Maybe even say she's coming home.

I wait.

I try again.

"I was thinking you could talk to him."

"He must have a good reason."

The M in the water ring starts to disappear. "Help him to understand."

"Melina, I'm not communicating with your dad right now, and I'm opposed to taking sides. You're smart. You're brilliant. I'm sure you can figure this out by yourself." Her voice, firm and unyielding, seems to echo throughout the empty house.

"By myself?" I say. "What you really mean is alone. I'm left to go it alone."

At that, I hang up.

The evening before the dance, Dad still won't budge on Marcus. It's ridiculous. He's never been like this before. Finally, I come up with a way around him, but it will only work with Lyde's help. Everything depends on him.

"Please, Lyde?" I hold tight to my phone, go out into the backyard and walk in circles.

"I don't know."

"It won't take long. Ten minutes tops and then you'll be on your way." I step over the sprinkler hose.

"Still, though, Melina, flat out deceive your dad?"

"Listen, it's not really deceiving him. Dad's acting so weird right now. If things were normal, he wouldn't be like this."

"I'm rotten at lying."

"Come over tonight and we can practice."

"I can't. It's Wednesday and I've got youth group."

"Okay, I'll come with you then."

"You want to come to church and help me practice lying?"

"Sorry, I know that sounds bad." He doesn't say anything. "Lyde?" I wait. *Please, please, please.*

"Mel, are you sure?"

"Yes."

"He's worth all of this?"

71

"Please, will you do it for me?"

"I'll think about it," he says with a sigh.

Getting There

Of course, Dad doesn't care if I go to the dance with Lyde. He trusts Lyde like a collie. Peeking through the blinds, I check out the window and try to push away *los nervios* that are bubbling up inside of me. Still no truck. I go to my mirror and spin, watching my dress float.

I touch my hair, checking to see if the bobby pins I used are still there. Again and again, I look at the clock… five minutes after… six minutes. Lyde is never late. I sit on my bed and try to wiggle my toes inside the new cowboy boots I bought. The creamy brown leather accents my dress perfectly, but they're a half-size too small. It shouldn't matter for just one night.

Finally, I hear the crunch of tires on gravel and run to the window. There it is—the YO truck! A good, old dependable truck. A beautiful truck even if all the letters in Toyota are faded out except Y and O. Heat travels down my back and my sweat glands open, working double-time.

I reapply deodorant. I've got on three layers now, but they don't seem to be working. I grab a box of Kleenex and stuff wads of tissue in my pits.

After the doorbell rings, I take a breath, toss open my bedroom door and hurry down the hall to the living room, wobbling in the boots. "Hey," I say, trying to sound casual, normal, like I'm not a big, fat liar.

Dad and Lyde turn and stare.

"Mel… you're beautiful," says Dad, like he's seeing me for the first time.

Lyde nods, looking surprised too.

"You like the dress?" Bree found it. She got it from one of her acting friends who'd just finished doing *Oklahoma*. In the cowboy boots and flowing dress, I look like a country girl who's just stepped out of a field of sunflowers

"And hey, Lyde," I say. He looks so different. His curly hair is tamed down to wavy. In the embroidered shirt and bolo tie, he looks taller and older, like the perfect, gentleman cowboy.

Dad gives me a grin. But as I get closer, his grin fades and his forehead scrunches down.

Lyde scratches behind his ear.

Dad squints at me and frowns. Something's wrong.

This is it.

My mouth goes dry. "I, uh."

Dad shakes his head.

Somehow, he knows Lyde isn't my real date. Did Lyde tell him?

"Melina, what in the world?"

Dead, I am so dead.

Where do I start? *You don't understand. You gave me no choice.*

"Melina," says Dad.

"I'm sorry," I say.

He points to his armpit and whispers, "Your dress."

"My dress?" I look down. Sheets of Kleenex are poking out, exploding from under my arms. Oh! The tissues! He's frowning at the tissues!

"Oops." I grab each wad, untuck them from my dress, and stare at the tissue globs. "Um… it's a beauty secret. Bree told me all about… scented tissue instead of perfume. That way it's not too overpowering. These are…" I stare at the purple tissue. "Lilacs in Bloom." I stumble into the kitchen, toss the tissues in the garbage, and hurry back.

"Okay, now, let's get some photos," says Dad, and he goes into the kitchen for his phone. Sweat is starting to build up on Lyde's forehead and he tugs at his collar. He gets real close and whispers, "I hate lying."

"I'm sorry," I say, and I really am, but here we are right in the middle of this and what am I supposed to do?

When Dad gets back and points his phone at us, Lyde puts his arm around me. His arm and hand feel limp and clammy, like a whole row of dead fish against my skin. Dad takes picture after picture. The room turns into a sauna, and soon I'm going to need a whole box of Kleenex. "Dad, really we need to go."

"One more." He taps at his phone.

I grab Lyde's hand and pull him to the door.

"You look good together," says Dad as he follows us. "Back by midnight?"

Lyde turns. "Maybe earlier."

"Or later," I say.

"Okay, I'll plan on midnight," says Dad.

We walk outside and the cold wind hits my sweating body, and I start to get that sick-with-a-fever feeling. Dad stays and watches from the doorway. Lyde opens my door and I slide in. Once he's seated, he puts the key in the ignition but stops.

No Burger King bags at my feet. No rotten french fries or dirty plastic spoons. "You cleaned your car? She must be someone special," I say, hoping my teasing will smooth everything over.

"I almost didn't come in," he says, his voice low.

I thump my hand against my leg in a drumbeat. "I'm sorry. It's just that my dad's crazy right now. And I'm left alone to deal with it."

"We could go back. We could tell your dad there's been a mistake—that we're not going together."

"Lyde, please, I can't do that to Marcus," I plead.

"But you can do this to me?" He shakes his head and turns the key.

Harvest Dance

Lyde drops me off at the parking lot of Suds Car Wash, right where Marcus is waiting, standing outside his car. When I told Marcus I had to sneak around my dad, he said he understood. That now, whenever he meets with the Air Force recruiter, he tells his mom he's going to the batting cages.

I put my hand on Lyde's arm. "Hey. Thanks a lot," I say softly, knowing it isn't enough.

He stares straight ahead. I slip out the door, duck down and say, "Really, I owe you."

He doesn't move.

"Can we go to lunch tomorrow? At *El Mercado?* I'll get you all the Mexican pastries you can eat." And then I'll tell him how he's the greatest friend, and how he saved my life, and that I owe him forever. I'll do all of that—tomorrow.

I hurry over to Marcus. He waves at Lyde. "Thanks

dude," he calls out. But Lyde doesn't even look over as he drives away.

The dance is at The Red Barn just outside of town. We pull into the parking lot and the second Marcus and I get out of the car, we can hear the band fiddling their hearts out. Inside the barn, white lights drape down from the rafters and sunflowers decorate the tables. Hay bales are stacked along the sides for extra seating and there's a harvest moon photo backdrop. But most everyone is out dancing.

"Ready?" says Marcus. Before I shout *yes!*, so he can hear me over the music, he grabs me by the hand and we run out to the dance floor.

Suddenly, we're twisting, moving and twirling, as the band rocks the barn. A group in front of the stage starts a line dance: heel-toe, heel-toe, twist, turn to the side, clap. I actually know this one! A girl taught us one night at Lyde's church. "Come on." I try to pull Marcus into the dance line but he doesn't budge.

"Whoa, now," he says, giving me a crinkly-eye smile. "You're actually into this kind of stuff?"

"It's easy. Just follow me." Reluctantly, he lets me drag him into the line and the crowd fills in around us.

"I'll need your tutoring," he says. He watches a few steps, but soon he's stepping, kicking, and shuffling along with everyone. "I can't believe you talked me into this."

"Easy as pi, 3.14." I say with a grin.

He shakes his head. "Nice dad joke."

We dance in sync: hips swaying, shoulders dipping, feet shuffling. After a quick turn, he stumbles and bumps into me, knocking me to the side. Quickly he grabs my waist, steadying me. "Sorry there, Melina girl."

His hands are soft and warm and for a moment, he just holds me there and looks at me with those blue Jolly Rancher eyes. Heat from dancing, from his hands, from all corners of the barn, shoot through me like a furnace. We stay like that just a moment longer, until the guitarist gives the final strum, the drummer gives the last beat, and everyone erupts in an avalanche of applause.

On a stage up front, the fiddle player steps up to the microphone. "All righty now, after all that fancy footwork, we're going to slow things down a bit." The guitar player starts to strum a soft melody. A fog machine turns on and the whole dance floor turns into a puffy cloud.

Marcus pulls me close, and I wrap my arms around his neck. As we dance together, a wave of calm washes over me—the lying to Dad, messing up with Lyde —I push it all far away. And it's just us. Me—sinking deeper and deeper. And him—holding me tight. And we sway and I feel like I could stay right here, safe in his arms for hundreds and hundreds of songs.

Not until the music ends do we pull apart.

"I've been thinking," says Marcus.

"Hum?"

"We should do more dancing and less studying."

"I think you're right, Air Force."

"Let me see if I can find us a drink," he says and before I can say, *I'll go with you*, he disappears in the fog and I'm there on the dance floor alone.

The band starts again and I scoot off. The too-small boots rub tight. My heels and the sides of my feet are starting to feel tender. I try sitting on one of the hay bales, but the straw pokes into my legs, so I move to a chair.

In a flash of flowing curls under a cowboy hat, here comes Bree. She looks one-hundred-percent countrified in her white cotton dress. I bounce up and am about to hug her, but as she gets closer—she's got this look on her face.

Instead of hugging, I want to run in the opposite direction. "How's my hair? Is it okay?" I ask, trying for a distraction.

"*Cielos chica*, what happened?"

"Happened?" I fake like I don't know what she's talking about.

"Your hair is stunning. But *madre mía*, I just saw Lyde. He looks pale and grouchy. When I asked him if he'd seen you, he just shook his head and walked away."

"Lyde. Where's Lyde?" I pop up on my tiptoes, but it makes my feet ache even worse.

"Mel, come on. What happened?"

I blow out a breath. "Well, you know how my dad has been super crazy and how he flipped out."

"Okay?"

"Who else could I call last minute to be my fake date?"

"*Madre mía,*" she says again.

"If I hadn't, I wouldn't be here. I'd be at home googling: *How to place a gypsy curse.*

"You and Lyde, both of you lied right to his face?" She bites her lip like she's trying to hold in a million and one Spanish words she'd like to yell at me.

But she doesn't get it. She doesn't understand how different things are at home. How off everything is. "Come on, Bree, we're at this great dance and you look gorgeous." I hold onto her wrists.

She takes a strand of my hair and retwists it around her finger. "Well, you did do a fabulous job on your hair."

"And where's your date? The guy from stage crew, right?"

Bree nods over to the refreshment table. Her date is basketball-player tall and blond. He's piling up lemon squares and white powdered cookies. "Yeah, he was right under my nose. Though technically, he was on top of a ladder, fixing the lighting."

I look for Marcus but can't see him anywhere. On the other side of the room, couples stand in line to get their pictures taken in front of a harvest moon backdrop. Lyde waits with his date, and even from across the room in dim light, I can tell she looks amazing, in a flowing dress with her long auburn hair. The band starts in on their third song since Marcus walked away.

"Where's Marcus? He should be back by now."

"Isn't he?" Bree nods towards the crowd.

"Dancing? No," I say. "Definitely not." Marcus wouldn't be out there without me. Bree's right about all kinds of stuff, about hair and clothes and even eyeliner, but sometimes she's dead wrong. I check out where she's looking and, of course, there's nothing. Of course, she's wrong.

The band plays a country classic, a heart-wrencher. The kind with a surprise ending that makes you want to bawl your eyes out. I stretch up, straining to see. Everyone is so jumbled together, but I catch something… A glimpse of something… That color of shirt… I stare and the sea of people parts… until right there are those solid shoulders, swaying to the music, with someone's hands wrapped around him.

I close my eyes. Wishing a blink would reset everything. Control-Alt-Delete what's happening right in front of me. But there they are, Marcus and Kensly. Kensly, wearing a Daisy Duke dress. And the two of them, dancing so close, there's not even a breath of air between them.

Heat rises from my stomach, burning my face, and air sticks in my lungs. My words fumble out. "I thought he was…" His hands slide around her waist. Hers slide all over him.

I back up and slump right there on one of the chairs that ring the barn. An outside chair, a non-dancing chair, a wall-flower chair. Bree sits down by me. "*Oye*, maybe it's different than it looks. Maybe they're…"

I try not to look. "Didn't he say he was going to get a drink?"

"…just good friends," says Bree.

And I stay like that until the song finishes with a final staccato beat. Then I stand up and I'm marching out of there, in those too-tight cowboy boots, with the straw under my feet.

"*Híjole g*irl, where are you going?"

"Out."

After the Dance

If only I could trade these stupid boots for some running shoes. I push through the crowd, rush out the barn and into the dark night.

"Mel…" Bree's at my side, doing a shuffle-run, trying to keep up. "Hold up."

"An idiot! How could I be such an idiot?"

She grabs my arm. "You're not. He's the *imbécil*."

"I thought…" I shake her hand off and keep going, pounding at the ground. What did I think? That we had something together. The two of us. All the studying. Laughing. Going out for food. To the movies. I thought all those things meant something. That they added up to a relationship.

"Slow down," she says, breathing hard. "We're not all runners."

I slow but keep a steady pace. The boots rubbing against my feet.

"Forget that *payaso, el tonto*. It's cold out. Let's go inside, find Lyde, and we'll all hang out together."

No way am I going back in there. No way am I going to sit around and watch someone else walk out on me.

She turns. "I need to go tell…"

"Bree, you go back. Stage crew guy is probably looking all over for you."

"Melina!" someone calls. It's Marcus standing back at the barn. He starts jogging over.

"Really, I'm fine." I grab Bree's hands. "Go back to the dance. I just need some air. I'll see you soon." It's a lie. A big one. But I'm not going to ruin Bree's night.

"See you in a few?" says Bree.

"Yes, for sure."

"Wait, Melina." Marcus catches up.

I keep pounding at the ground, trying to get away. He matches my footsteps.

"Hey, hold up. Where are we going?" He wipes sweat off his forehead. Sweat from dancing with her.

"Home."

"We're going home already?" he asks.

Thump. Thump. I pound at the ground. Every step hurts. "No, *I'm* walking home." The gravel parking lot ends. I cross the street and keep going, rushing down the narrow, country road. Marcus follows.

"It's at least ten miles to your house."

"Ten miles is nothing. It's an easy Saturday run." Though these tight boots will make it painful.

"Melina, please—my grandpa would kill me if he finds out I let you walk home alone."

It's a solid no-moon-out dark. A car comes speeding up behind us. I move into the weeds and keep going. The car zips by, blowing my hair back and pelting us with dirt.

"Wait just a minute. I'll be right back," says Marcus.

No way am I falling for that again. It was burning up inside the barn, but now outside it's cool. I'll be freezing and my feet covered in blisters by the time I'm home but I don't care. Headlights come from behind. An engine hums. Marcus appears driving alongside me, rolling the passenger window down.

"Melina, please. I'll drive you home, okay?"

My feet are red hot.

"Kensley asked me to dance, okay? What was I supposed to do, be a total jerk and tell her no?"

I walk faster, trying to warm up. Of course, she'd be pushy like that. Godzilla Kensley, the soccer player. A car behind Marcus blares its horn. He waves them on. They swerve around and once they're in front, the driver hits the gas. Tires squeal and tiny rocks go flying.

"Melina, this is dangerous. Please."

I keep going.

"Okay, we'll walk then." He drives to clearing up ahead,

pulls over, parks, then comes running back. "Look Melina, Kensley is going through a lot at home. Last year, we were together all the time. When I had to leave, I broke it off. She took it really hard. So, when she asked me to dance as friends… I said yes. I shouldn't have, but I did."

"Friendly dancing?" I kick at the weeds.

Marcus bends down, picks up a rock, and pitches it into the night. "When she started putting her hands all over me, I knew it was wrong. I knew I'd messed up. And then I saw you leave… and geez, I'm sorry. I always mess things up. Why do I always mess things up?"

With each step, my foot rubs against the boots. Dad and Lyde—I messed up with both of them tonight. I didn't mean to but I had.

"I asked you to the dance. I wanted to be with you."

It's true. He waited at my locker and asked me. Not her. He's always with me. At least three times a week to study and every Friday night, he's with me. And now, am I just being like my parents, really stubborn and messing up everything good?

We've walked until we're next to his car. He reaches over, gently slips his hand into mine. Around us the stars have started to pop out, and here, away from all the city lights they glow big and bright and beautiful. He squeezes my hand.

"Sorry I messed up."

I shrug. "It happens."

He smiles. "Not with you, Melina girl. You're the least messed-up person I know."

I laugh and shake my head. "Then, you don't know me that well."

"I don't know everything. But I bet you could go for a strawberry milkshake right now."

I laugh. "True."

"Come on. Let's go get some food."

We get in the car and he drives, easing onto the country road. Slowly passing empty fields. Slowly heading toward town. He passes me his phone and says, "Here, pick us some music."

I scroll through his playlists.

"What do you think, best burgers and shakes in town?"

"Well, you know… they probably won't let you in."

"Why not?"

"When they see how slow you drive, they'll tell you to go McDonald's because you don't belong at Zips."

He smiles. "Nice one."

The River

Halfway through the perfect burger, dripping with melty cheese, I ask, "So… how did the polynomial test go?"

"Seriously, Melina?" Marcus puts his hand to his chest like an offended, hankie-holding, old lady. "We're on a date. I don't want to even think about school." He leans forward grinning and says, "But I did get a ninety-five."

"Nice!" I say, dipping a fry in the sauce.

When we've finished our milkshakes and have eaten everything but petrified, french-fry crumbs, we take off. We take the long way, driving along the Kennewick side of the river, where you're right next to the deep purple water and can watch all the lights dancing on the ripples.

"I'm so ready to move out and start my own life, but you know, I might miss this," I say.

"There is something about it. Isn't there?" He reaches over and holds my hand. "Like you. There sure is something about you, Einstein Girl." As our fingers lock together, my heart slams around in my chest, like I'm some little junior high girl who's never held hands before. *I have— it's just been a long time.* We cruise along until the end of the road, then we head back to Pasco.

"You know, you never told me. Where did you disappear to last year?"

He blows out a breath. "Well, that is a very unlucky story."

I nod and think about my own unlucky stories.

"My dad took off."

"Moved to another town?"

"Nope, one night he just never came home from work."

"What do you mean?"

"He disappeared. Couldn't find him anywhere. His business partner didn't know where he'd gone to. His phone no longer worked. His credit cards weren't being used. It was like he'd been abducted by aliens, which, actually, was one of my mom's theories."

"*Híjole.*"

"She thought up all kinds of stupid scenarios. Maybe he started working with the CIA and that's why he disappeared. Or maybe he'd been kidnapped. Or maybe he was that anonymous guy who won the mega lottery and he was waiting until all the press died down to show up and tell us about it. She took me out of school and we traveled around searching for him."

"And you found him?"

"No. Finally, a month later, his business partner found him. Said he'd bankrupted the business, was living in Mexico and wasn't coming back."

"Oh, my. I'm really sorry," I say.

He shrugs. "You know, you think your parents are great. They're like gods or something and then when they mess up so bad, it's like you don't know what to believe in anymore."

I squeeze his hand. "I know. My mom took off three months ago. Just packed her bags and left." I haven't told anyone besides Bree and Lyde.

"See," he says. "And when crap like that happens, what do you believe in?"

I don't say anything. Because I don't know who to believe in either.

Marcus doesn't take the turn to my house but keeps driving. "You don't have to go home yet, do you?"

I check the time on my phone. It's past midnight. Dad will be up, waiting for the sound of my key in the lock. I know all about that waiting, straining to hear that sound. But I don't want to go home and sit in the dark and wish for something that's not going to happen. "I'm fine. I have time," I say. There's a bunch of texts from Bree I didn't see before.

where r u?

still looking for you
what's going on?
Mel??

MEEEELL!

what the heck Mel? I'm the one who loses my phone, not you. You better not be dead.

Quickly I answer. *SOOOOO SORRY! I'm fine. I'm fine. with Marcus. call u soon. :)*

He turns down the road to Chiawana Park and as we drive, it's like we're entering a different world. Giant trees line the road, towering above us, making a shadowy canopy. Acres and acres of grass spread out like a welcome mat, and straight ahead there's the massive Columbia River.

Of course, everything looks different in the dark, but I've been here so many times I could walk around with my eyes closed. The play areas with swing sets. The giant tractor tires for hiding in. "See that slide," I say, pointing to a thin tall shadow. "I remember being too scared to go down that. And that…" I point to the rectangle shadowed area, "We've done bunches of barbeques there." We pull up to the parking lot, but there's a thick metal rope hung across the entrance. A closed sign hangs in the middle. "We're too late."

"We're dreamers. We're not giving up that easily." Marcus drives down the boat launch road and parks by a couple of trucks with empty boat trailers.

We walk the bike path. My boot-rubbed feet ache but I ignore them. In the distance I can see the blue bridge and the lights of cars passing over. We bump arms and this time, I slip my hand in his. He raises our hands up and kisses my hand; suddenly I feel like I'm on a tilt-a-whirl.

"See that light?" He points with his free hand. A red light rotates around and around on the very top of the bridge. "It's to warn the pilots as they fly in."

"Someday it will be you flying over the bridge," I say.

"And you'll be the famous biologist, flying first class, coming to visit the river."

"Come on," I say, as I pull him through a path worn in the grass. We thud up wooden planks, until we stand on a wobbling dock. The lights from the houses across the river shimmer in long wavy triangles on the water.

"Nice view?" I ask.

"Beautiful," he says looking directly at me.

The dock sways, he pulls me close and wraps his arms around me. His arms, warm and solid, press against my skin where my dress scoops low. I lean into him and my lips find his. And that tilt-a-whirl feeling goes airborne. Rising higher, higher than any light on any bridge in any town.

We stay like that until a breeze starts and a cold shiver runs through me. He pulls away and rubs my arms. "You've got goosebumps," he says. "Let's get you warm."

When we get to his car, he opens the trunk. "I've got workout clothes." He flashes me a goofy grin. "Clean ones."

He hands me a sweatshirt and some sweat pants and grabs himself some too. Before I know it, Marcus strips out of his western shirt and Wranglers. "I've been stuck in these stiff clothes for too long."

Oh my! Boxers! Marcus stands next to me in boxer. Heat shoots up through my gut and burns my face. He pulls on the sweat pants and then looks at me. His chest, shoulders, arms, naked. Staring... is rude. But right now, I don't care.

"Do you need help?" He grins, pulling on a T-shirt.

I blink. "Some privacy."

"Gotcha. I'll wait over there."

My heartbeat thunders away. I slip off the boots and my toes sing out *Hallelujah*. I pull the sweatpants up under my dress and roll the waistband three times. I unzip my dress with trembling hands and shimmy it over my head, then hold it in front of me, covering my bra. "You're staying away, right?"

"Yes, ma'am." His voice sings out from over by the trees.

I quickly slide on the sweatshirt and then Marcus jogs back. He starts digging around in the trunk. He pulls out a blanket, two cups, a bottle of wine, and a speaker.

"No spare tire and jack?" I laugh.

"I only bring the important stuff," he says.

He hands me the blanket and looks down at my feet.

Oh no, please, not my massive blistering feet. Carefully, I place one foot on top of the other, trying to hide them.

"There might be glass around. I'll carry you." He hoists me up like I weigh nothing and carries me piggyback, all the way down until we're right on the river's edge. Then he eases me down. I grab the corners of the blanket and let it float down. My heart pounds to the thumping of his feet, as he runs back and returns with the speaker and wine. Marcus opens the wine and pours it into two cups. He gives me one and holds up the other. "To us on this special night."

Sure, I've had a little wine on Christmas and New Year's, and tonight feels just like that, a special occasion.

"To us," I say, sipping. It's fruity and smooth. We connect my phone to his speaker and dance right there next to the river. Lights flicker in the water as we sway. We stop and he pours more wine.

He tries to hand me the cup. It's super late by now. Him. Me. Dancing so close. It's a little too much. Maybe I should have him take me home. "I don't know," I say to the cup.

"No more?" asks Marcus. He drinks his, sets the cups down on the grass and then wraps me up in his arms. "I could stay here like this all night."

Dad can wait. Going home can wait. All I've been doing for weeks, even months now is waiting. I won't do it anymore.

We dance some more. And drink some more.

I hold Marcus tight as we dance and it feels like a dream. When the song is over, Marcus keeps hold of my hand, sits on the blanket and pulls me down next to him. We kiss for forever. When he slides his hands underneath the sweatshirt, onto my flaming hot skin, I know that tonight is special. Skin on skin. Me and the breeze, and Marcus. That's all there is. All that matters.

Going Home

We hold hands across the gap between the bucket seats. At the stoplight, he lets go and double grips the steering wheel. "I didn't know… that you hadn't…"

"You're my first serious relationship," I say, smiling. He reaches for my hand again and I hold it tight like it's a life raft.

When we get close, I have him stop a few doors down from my house. And then, like a common burglar, I creep along in the dark, clutching my wadded-up dress and the cowboy boots. In Dad's bedroom window, I can see the light glowing from the TV. *Stay there. Stay where you are.*

The porch light shines down like a pointing finger and my hand shakes. As I fit the key into the lock, it makes the loudest click. The sound echoes through the night and I imagine the neighbor lady yelling out her window, *What's going on? Who is that?* Quickly, I push the door open, slide through the gap and softly shut the door behind me, my heart slamming away. I do a quick-step down the hall on the balls of my feet.

A boot slips from my hands.

THUMP.

"Melina?"

I leave the boot and dash down the hallway into my room. I toss down my dress and the single boot, and jump into the bed, pulling the covers way up.

Seconds later, my door swings open. "Melina? When did you get in?"

I keep my eyes half-shut and pray that all those times I practiced Bree's lines with her will count for something. "Oh, hey Dad," I say in my sleepiest voice.

"You didn't tell me you were back."

I yawn, turn on my side, mumble, "Oh, sorry." I wait, my heartbeat pounding in my ears, willing my breath to slow down.

I wait.

And wait.

Finally, the door clicks shut.

And I stay there in bed. A big, fat liar.

Morning

"Piping hot strawberry crepes, almost ready," calls Dad.

Ugh. I bury my head under my pillow. When I peek out, there are Marcus's sweats right on the floor where I dropped them last night. I smile, remembering the dancing, the kisses, how he held me so close, like he would never let me go.

But everything—all of it. It was too much. I didn't plan on so much. I jump up and throw his clothes in my closet. The smell of crepes and strawberries is strong. My stomach rumbles and folds around like it's not sure what it wants.

"Ready," calls Dad.

I stumble through the hall, yanking down my pajama shirt.

"Glad to see you up." He digs his spatula into the pan.

I rub my eyes. The Sunday morning routine; Dad's back at it. We haven't done this since Mom left. Dad pours me a tall glass of orange juice. "I have one quick house showing today, a nice Cape Cod close to the river. Though it's not on a cul-de-sac. Everyone wants a cul-de-sac these days."

"Hmm," I say. Outside, the leaves dance in the wind.

Dad hands me crepes. The plate radiates heat and, all piled up, the crepes look like layers of skin.

"Cul-de-sacs and new carpeting," he says, pouring his juice. "Now, tell me about the dance."

I shrug. "No big deal. Just a dance."

"Who was the band?"

"I'm not sure."

"Lyde got you home later than I thought."

"Um." I nod and take another bite so I don't have to say a thing.

Later, in the early afternoon, I stretch out on a blanket in the backyard with textbooks. I've got calculus, advanced biology, physics, and an essay for English I need to catch up on. But all I can think about is last night: the river, the dancing, the kissing, the skin on skin.

My phone rings. I grab it fast, but it's not Marcus. "Oh hey."

"*Cada cosita.* You have to tell me every little thing!" says Bree.

Does she know about last night, somehow? Does my voice sound different?

101

"I've been wanting to call you all morning, but I couldn't during church. Did you kick his butt all the way to California, or what?"

She doesn't know, and I can't tell her. Years ago, in junior high, Bree and I made a pact. She got a purity ring from her church and made a vow not to have sex until marriage. She told me she promised God and everything. I told her I thought it was cool and I promised her I'd wait until I found the right guy in college. And we kind of made a big thing about it. We blew out candles and made promises on the Bible. And now I can't tell her I broke that pact.

She won't get it. Marcus and I are good together. We go for nachos and every time we're there, he scoops up his jalapeños and puts them right on top of my chips, because he knows I like them so much.

"At the dance, it was just a misunderstanding."

"*Cómo?*"

"Marcus dancing without me. I was wrong. It was all a mistake."

"But we saw Marcus and Kensly together."

"Yeah, but we were wrong about it. She asked him and he was just being a friend. It was no big deal."

"*Híjole girl*, I don't—"

"Really, it's fine. We talked it all out."

"Hum… So, what happened? Where did you go after the dance?"

102

"Just around," I say. "Out for frozen yogurt." I hate lying to Bree. But the more I talk, the more I have to lie. "Well, sorry, I've got to run. My dad and I, we've got this thing. Let me call you back."

"What thing?" she asks, sounding suspicious.

Quickly, I say, "Love ya! See ya!"

As soon as I'm done with Bree, I punch in Marcus's number.

It goes straight to voicemail.

I don't leave a message. I just hang up. His grandpa probably has him moving sprinkler pipe. It's a huge job, hooking up pipe to a four-wheeler, dragging it to another spot, going back for more. All that back and forth, it's a lot. He's told me all about his demanding grandpa. It's okay. I can wait.

Later, I call again and text him, too. But still… nothing. A tiny corner of my heart starts to worry and bite its nails. It's not until the sun is going down and our giant cottonwood trees cast shadows on our house that I get a text from Marcus.

hey some chickens escaped. been busy looking everywhere. I think they dug under the fence and then flew off like they were crazy for freedom or something. gotta run. C u 2mrw.

I smile and tell that corner of my heart: *See, I told you so.*

Monday

Overnight, a storm blows in, turning everything frosty. I pull my jacket tight but still arrive at school shivering. At my locker, I move all my books to the bottom, because maybe Marcus will want to put his books and notebooks in here.

I search the crowd, but I don't see him. The halls start to fill up but no camouflage backpack, no Air Force sweatshirt. I stand on my tiptoes and search. *Nada*. But then, there in the crowd, there's Lyde. And seeing him, the way he smiles at everyone, it makes my stomach drop. I didn't call him or text him or thank him. What I really need to do is apologize. "Hey Lyde," I call out.

When Lyde sees me, his smile fades. He nods but stays way over on the other side of the hall. The crowd carries him down the hall like a fast-moving river, and the ache in my stomach feels like it's being slammed with a crowbar.

The warning bell rings. I do my fastest walk-but-not-run through the halls. All around, lockers keep slamming, the sound ringing through the school. When I turn the corner, there's Marcus's locker, fourth from the end. But the whole row is empty.

After two breaks between classes and still no sign of Marcus, I go to my locker and shove my books on the shelf that I saved for him. Whatever. It doesn't matter. I'm not worried. Marcus probably slept in. No biggie. Or maybe he's still out chasing chickens or harvesting alfalfa. It doesn't mean anything. I grab my calculus book.

And then I remember. It's Monday—quiz day—and I haven't even looked at Friday's notes. Quick-fast, I grab my binder and rush off. If I get there early, I'll have time to study. I barrel down the hall and slip around the corner so fast I collide into some guy.

"Hey, watch it!" He flips around. It's Frank, and right next to him is Marcus.

"Marcus?" I say, like it's a question and lined up behind it are a whole bunch more questions, like where have you been, and is everything okay, and please, please, please let everything be okay because I can't handle if they're not.

"Oh, hey, Einstein girl," says Marcus. The three guys all stand there at Tyrell's locker staring down at me.

"Hey… there… Marcus," I stammer. "What's going on? Do you want to go to lunch?"

He looks at the guys, and they're all standing there

105

weirdly quiet. "Sure. Let's do lunch. But don't you have class right now?"

"I haven't even studied, so I can miss."

"I don't want to be responsible for you getting an A-minus or something. Let's go grab something later, okay?" Tyrell pulls out his jacket and he and Frank rush down the hall. Marcus turns to go. "See you soon."

He flashes me that smile. It's a winning smile, an everything-is-okay smile, but there's something behind that smile I can't figure out.

The Shed

I click the remote, shuffling through TV shows, but everything looks dumb. I check my phone again. No text. No call.

Out in the carport, Dad plays the piano. Tonight, it's Beethoven, and he's turned all of the sonatas into weepy ones that sound like they were made for funerals. I check my phone again.

I called Marcus two hours ago, and his mom answered his phone. "What?" she said, sounding like I tore her away from painting her nails or something. But when she realized who I was, she talked on and on about how we had to keep Marcus from enlisting in the Air Force.

When I pull my binder out of my backpack, the cover falls off. I grab my jacket and go out into the carport. Dad is so into his music, he's playing with his eyes closed.

"I need to go to the store. I'll be back soon, okay?"

His fingers fly up and down the keyboard, and he nods.

107

I'm not sure if it's to the beat of the song or to me, but I take it as—*go ahead*.

At Fred Meyer, I find the perfect binder, reinforced sides, double-strength pockets. When I go to check out, I grab a couple of Reese's, Marcus's favorite. I pay and then hurry out into the night.

As I'm driving away, it occurs to me that Marcus can't be moving irrigation line in the dark. I make an impulsive decision and drive out west of town, passing alfalfa fields and apple orchards. When I get to his farm, I turn onto their bumpy dirt road, and as I get closer to the big house, I flip off the headlights and crawl along in the dark. I don't want his grandparents coming out. Slowly, I drive the dirt road that circles the place. At the house in the back, I stop and park. Through the window, I can see a flickering light from the TV and a big-haired shadow sitting on the couch. Out front is his mom's sedan but no blue hatchback. No Marcus.

Slam. I pound my fist on the steering wheel. Where is he? He isn't avoiding me, is he? He wouldn't do that, would he? I yank down the gearshift and keep driving. The car bumps and dips and shakes on that lousy farm road.

My tire sinks into a hole and I gun it until I'm out. Then I hit a rock, bounce along and there's this *woosh* sort of sound and a *whapwhapwhapwhap* and the steering's off and… oh crap, what did I do? I can feel it. The car isn't right. It's thumping along. I stop, get out, and walk around. The tire's flat as anything. I run back to the driver's door and get my phone. Dead. It's still dead. I forgot. My charge cord has been blinking out, sometimes working and sometimes not. I throw my phone down on the seat.

It's dark and creepy outside, with a few haunted-looking trees around. But up farther, there's a light or something and a big rectangle shadow. I get in my car and slowly ease down the road, carefully dodging the holes. I get closer and can see that the shadow is a giant shed building, and there it is, parked outside—Marcus's car! Of course, he's probably out here working on a tractor or taking inventory of feed bags or something. Of course, now we'll be able to talk. Of course, he'll know how to change a tire.

I stop in the middle of the farm road, park, and grab the Reeses off the seat, throw open my door, and run toward the shed. Above the shed door, a dusty light barely glows like it's lighting my way.

The door falls open and I step into the darkness. It smells like dirt and grime, like potatoes and car oil. Carefully, I slide my feet along the floor, heading to the light ahead. I hold tight to the candy, knowing my eyes will soon adjust. I hear Marcus and I'm about to call out to him, to yell and say, *Hey, guess who?* But then I hear another voice, a female voice.

"Hold on. I think I hear something. Someone's here."

"Stop worrying. It's just us, babe."

I freeze. A shiver runs up my arms and explodes through my body. I shift from one foot to the other, trying to see. The shed is a giant maze: four-wheelers on one side, a feed pillar in front of me, all kinds of machine parts piled behind me.

Someone giggles.

Marcus's voice cuts through the dark. "Don't worry, we're alone."

I can't breathe. I squeeze the candy bars and scoot around burlap bags, feeling my way with my hand. A few yards away, a hanging light bulb sways. It lights up dust particles in the air and a workbench stacked with tools.

And Marcus. My Marcus.

All tangled up with someone. Someone who isn't me. My heart waits. The breeze from the open door dies. The light stops swaying. I stand there in suffocating stillness.

Nothing moves. Except for them. Underneath the light, he's kissing Kensly the way he kissed me.

My trembling hand pushes the hair out of my eyes, while his hands slide along her back, then rise up and remove the headband from her hair.

"Oh." The sound escapes from me and I drop the candy. They turn and look at me with big blank eyes.

I stumble through the shed, banging my shin against something, but I keep going. Outside, I keep running until

I fall into the car and I fumble, trying to get my key out of my pocket and then shove it into the ignition. I crank the ignition, hit the gas, and then *whumpwhumpwhump*. The tire! I don't care. I hold tight to that steering wheel and I keep the car steady. I wish I could squeal out of there. But I drive slowly down the road. Just away. I have to get away.

I ease down that awful dirt road and then, a few yards away, turn onto the regular asphalt road. I go a few more yards and then pull over onto the gravel shoulder. I pound the steering wheel again and again and again. I close my eyes. All I see is the two of them pressed together. His hands in her hair, his body all tangled up with hers.

Marcus with Kensly.

Just like at the Harvest Dance.

He said it was just a simple dance with her, but it wasn't.

It was a simple dance with me.

WINTER

Dumb

At the library, I find the SAT study guide section and pile thick books as high as my chin. I get out my laptop and download all the free SAT study guides. I have a new plan: a Forget-All-About-Him Plan. I'll study hard for the SAT. I'll ace all my classes. Everything will fall back into place. I'll get that scholarship to Portland State University, go out and get that degree in biology.

Marcus was a mistake. A pointless mistake. It was so dumb. Like forgetting to equal out both sides of the equation dumb. Like forgetting where oxygen is on the periodic table dumb. Like falling for a guy who only wanted free tutoring and a hookup dumb.

I know all about equations and quadrants and finding X for Y. But I couldn't see him and Kensly right in front of me.

Fine. Whatever. I won't be dumb anymore.

At Work

I drag through school like cement has been poured into my body and left to harden, trudging through class after class. When I get home, I plop onto my bed, open my binder, and try studying. But my eyelids are so heavy, letters and numbers of the formulas start blurring together, looking like Japanese, and I can't read Japanese so I put my head down and close my eyes.

A light flashes on and I blink at the light.

"Hey kiddo, I'm going out for some groceries," says Dad. "Can I get you something?"

My mouth feels sticky. The walls seem all wavy.

"There's tamale pie from last night in the fridge. Also, don't forget you need to clean the office tonight."

"It's dark?" I say, not believing what I can see out my window. I feel like I've been in some kind of a time warp.

"You've slept the afternoon away."

I eat the leftovers, drive to work, and drag up the stairs. The glass doors at Best Life Realty are spotted with fingerprints. Why can't people use the handle, instead of messing up the glass with their grimy hands? Inside, the wastebaskets are overflowing; someone has left a trail of tiny paper-punched circles that winds to the copy machine; and the kitchen is filled with crumbs, plates, and cups from someone's birthday party.

I decide to start with the dishes, then finish everything else and empty the dishwasher. I rinse out a coffee mug with a dumb joke about PMS and set it in the dishwasher. Maybe that's the reason I feel so awful, PMS. It's about time, isn't it? I start counting back the weeks.

A really awful thought tries to force itself into my mind, but I won't let it. I'll start my period any day. If I'm late, it's because of stress. Studying for the SAT, getting my grades up at school, and everything with Marcus; I've been super stressed—that throws off your cycle. Stress messes everything up.

Courage

Bree slumps against the row of lockers while she waits for me. "Auditions are tomorrow and I'm not ready. Can you come over and read the part of the lion?"

"Theyyyyyyy're great!" I say, pointing a finger to the sky.

She rolls her eyes. "That's a cereal-eating tiger, not a lion."

"Same animal family."

"It's more like: *Put 'em up, put 'em up! Which one of you first?*" She raises her fists. "*I'll fight you both together if you want. I'll fight you with one paw tied behind my back.*"

"Oh, sure, *The Wizard of Oz*. I can do that." I grab my backpack, slam my locker shut, and head towards the stairwell. "This way is faster."

She gives me a look. "It's not faster."

"Come on," I say, pleading.

"Are you seriously going to walk the long way around forever?"

"Not forever." I hoist my backpack up on my shoulder. "Just until I graduate."

She raises her eyebrows at me.

"I don't care how long it's been. I'm not going anywhere near his locker."

"What if there's a fire?"

"A fire, the roof collapsing, poisonous snakes, I'll still go the long way around."

"How about some courage?" she says, as she follows me.

"That's for lions."

Outside, the wind blows hard and rotten leaves crunch under our feet. Lyde is up ahead, getting into his truck. "Hey!" I yell, wishing he would come over and maybe we could go to El Mercado and hang out together. But he waves and ducks into his car. Ever since the harvest dance, things have been different between us. He's been busy hanging out with that redhead, hardly has time for me anymore.

Bree digs through her backpack. "Hold on. I left my script in the locker. I'll be right back." She runs back into the school, but I keep walking to her car.

"Melina!" someone calls out. I know the voice. And for the tiniest second, it's like the neurons in my brain misfire, and I forget everything and instead feel excited. And it's so wrong, so wrong because that stupid voice is Marcus.

I lean against Bree's car and hold my backpack in front of me as Marcus jogs over.

"Hey," he says.

"What?"

He stuffs a fist into his pocket. "Just, you know, how's it going?"

"Fine," I say, sounding as unfine as possible. The wind blows my hair into my face, and I brush it away and look at everyone else jumping into cars and zooming off. Where's Bree? Or Lyde? Or anyone who can come and take me away?

"I wanted to tell you. I got my AFQT scores back. You know, the test for the Air Force?"

I blink.

"I scored in the top ten percent. It's a huge win. I'll get in easy and be able to choose from a bunch of different careers. So I wanted to say thanks. You know, for helping me."

I don't know what to say, so I settle for nothing.

He looks down. "And, well, I thought we were just relaxed. You know, nothing serious."

"Really?" I clutch my backpack tighter. "You really think that none of that was serious?"

He sticks his fist in his pocket. "You know, high school's just casual, right?"

I shake my head in disbelief. Us studying together three

120

days a week wasn't just something casual. Me not keeping my grades up in my classes so I could help him instead wasn't casual either. And us together, on that blanket down by the river—that was the least casual of all. The wind whips and twirls and blows around me like a hurricane. "No. It wasn't casual to me."

He studies the ground, bites his lip, and then whispers, "Sorry." Then he shrugs and takes off.

I grab the car handle, fling open the door, and fall inside.

Shopping

I'm back at work Wednesday night, feeling sick and hollow, like the wind could pick me up, and toss me around. When I'm finally finished, I wrap the cord around the vacuum cleaner and heave all the trash bags out to the dumpster. As I slide into my car, everything starts spinning.

Something's wrong. For a week, I've been running to the bathroom to check, waiting for my period, but nothing. It can't be *that*, there's no way it's *that*. But I'm driving by Fred Meyer, and I realize—if I take one test, I can relax. No more counting weeks. No more worrying.

When I walk inside, a sales lady looks at me and glances at her watch. No need to worry, I want to tell her. I won't be long.

I stare straight ahead and grab a basket. A woman leans over the jewelry case, peering inside, but no one else is around. I walk down the main row, tossing things, any kinds of things, into my basket. I don't see the pregnancy tests yet. Down one row, a clerk arranges the toothpaste in nice, straight lines.

I hurry, passing by soap, zit cream, lotion. I pass by more and more rows: razors, shaving cream. And then, finally, there they are, next to the maxi pads, boxes of tests. All with neon lettering, pulsing out: Answer—Easy—Fast.

That toothpaste clerk is three rows away. No one else is around. I could stuff the box into my jacket, but that would be dumb. I grab the closest test. My pulse pounds faster than any of my runs. I push the test to the bottom of the basket. Cover it with all the other junk and speed to the checkout.

The woman is waiting by the registers. "I'll ring you up on four," she says, sounding tired.

I hand over the basket and watch her fingers as she scans the purchases: vitamin C, tampons, men's hair dye. I can feel sweat seeping out above my lip, and I wipe it away.

Her fingers dip into the basket, then scan. Dip, then scan. The scanner's red light reads the bars on a tube of Chapstick. All of a sudden, I feel hot, middle-of-July hot. Please, just finish fast. Two more things, then I'm gone—a box of Junior Mints, then finally the test. Sweat collects on the back of my neck. She picks it up, slides it across the scanner, and drops it into the shopping bag.

"Thirty-two fifty."

I hand her two twenties, get the change, and walk away,

half closing my eyes. Yes! I walk towards the door, wanting to click my heels together.

In and out, and no one knows what I have in my bag. Easy as a jog down to the river. Ten more steps and I'm outside.

Five steps.

Almost there.

Three steps.

"Excuse me," says a voice.

What?

I slow down and look around, dread rising in my chest.

"Hold on there, hon."

I stop. My stomach flips.

A yellow-vested woman walks over from the customer service desk. "Let me check your bags."

I stand there, paralyzed. My heart pauses in my chest and I can't breathe.

She takes the bag out of my hand. Looking inside, she shuffles things around. She pulls out the tampons and THE TEST. "Well, you won't be needing both."

Heat rushes up through me, and I cross my arms, sure my neck is turning splotchy red.

She studies me over her bifocals, leans in, and whispers. "It's the pregnancy test. A security officer saw you on that aisle. It always draws their attention. You wouldn't believe how many kids I catch stealing these things."

She takes the receipt out of my hand and looks it over. "Yer good."

I wish that the ceiling of Fred Meyer would collapse and bury me right there. She hands back the bag and places a warm hand on my arm. "Now, don't you worry. You'll be all right." She gives my arm a squeeze. "Everything will work out."

I drive home in a daze. I can't believe I just bought a pregnancy test—me! Me, the one who'd only kissed two guys before Marcus. Me, the one who made a pact with Bree.

My nose goes drippy. I look for a napkin or Kleenex or paper or anything to wipe my nose. But there's nothing. So, like a toddler, I use my sleeve, which makes me sniff harder. I can't be pregnant. I can't have a baby. I can't even take care of my own snot.

When I'm finally home, I tiptoe through the house and check. Dad is in bed, asleep. I lock the bathroom door, sit on the floor, and read all the directions—twice. Pretty much it says: pee on stick, then wait. One line: not pregnant. Two lines: pregnant. The printing makes it seem so easy. My life hinges on one line, one tiny half-inch line.

I pee, then set the timer on my phone... five minutes.

Sitting on the toilet lid, I press my balled-up fists into my eyelids. This can't be. This can't happen to me.

I pray. I do the whole thing like the preacher does at

Lyde's church, bow my head, clasp my hands, and then I whisper so quietly my prayer.

Please God, don't let me be pregnant. I can't have a baby. Please help me. I'll go back to church with Lyde. And I could learn to play that guitar that always sits on stage. I'll pray every day. Whatever I need to do, I'll do it. I won't ever be so stupid again or date stupid guys or do anything stupid. If I'm safe just this once. Please.

I wait.

And wait.

And I sit there listening to the drip, drip as the toilet tank refills.

The Answer

Two lines.

Pregnant.

Me.

I'm pregnant.

No. Wait. The test says it's 98% effective. There's a two percent chance. Maybe I'm the two percent. The plastic stick has to be wrong. I peed wrong.

But somewhere deep inside, I know it's not true. I'll take the second test in the box. And it will be the same as the first.

As I sit on the toilet, I have this feeling that if I look down, there will be nothing. The black and white tile I've padded around on since I was little will be gone. There'll be nothing but space.

I sit there until my legs go numb. Then I hear something in the kitchen. The cupboard door shuts. The squeak of the faucet handle. Water spilling out. A minute later, footsteps come towards the bathroom. My stomach surges.

"Melina? Are you okay?"

Okay? Am I okay?

The word sticks to my throat as it tries to come up. A word as dry as sand. "Yeah."

I'm fine. Just pregnant.

The cold tile shocks my feet. I hold onto the counter-top, steadying myself. Dad's footsteps thump as he goes back to his room. I grab up the test, the box, and the instructions and wrap everything in a towel and open the door. My bedroom seems a mile away, down the hallway. I tiptoe across the thin carpet all the way to my room, open my closet and bury the towel and evidence in the back corner, heaping dirty clothes on top.

I stumble across the floor, fall into bed and flip the comforter over me, making a cocoon. What I need is a cocoon, a reverse cocoon, one that will take me back in time. Back to my canopy bed, back to my blanket with the white eyelet lace, back and back and back.

"Hello?" Dad taps me on the arm.

"Sorry." I shake my head.

"I asked you three times already, what do you think about the sauce?"

128

I stare at my plate. Did I take a bite? Did I taste anything?

"It's a new recipe from this cooking-for-two website."

For two, two people. Now I'm two. I stare down, take my fork and pick at the chicken. The sauce is cloudy and hazy, a huge mess, and I don't even know what to say.

Someone kicks my leg. An achy pain shoots up from my shin. "Hey," I say.

Across the aisle, Bree is leaning over her desk, pulling her foot back. I rub my leg and stare at her in disbelief.

She whispers frantically, "He's been calling on you." She nods to the front of class, where Mr. Denslow is pointing at the whiteboard. "We'd like the answer today, Miss Abrums."

I blink. "Sorry… uh… sorry. What was the question?"

I lie on my bed, my knees tucked into my chest. Time pounds itself into my skin. It's so way down deep. Every second hammers. Tonight will be twenty-four hours since the test. I'm a ticking time bomb, and the alarm has been set.

I pull a blanket over me, bury deep under my pillow; if only I can sleep, go to that place of forgetting. My heartbeat pounds in my ears. I've done this before, so many times. I've stayed right here, trying not to listen to their fighting. I can't do it again. No! I shake and shake and shake my head. Then I throw off everything, the pillow, the blanket.

I grab my shoes off the floor, slip them on, and rush outside. The wind whips and whirls at me, but I don't care. I run across the driveway, down my street, passing house after house. The wind tries to push me back, but I run faster.

With each footstep, I pound at everything. Mom and Dad and their mess. Stupid, ridiculous Marcus and how I was dumb enough to help him study. And then, that night, at the river, I pound at that. And that horrible pregnancy test, I pound and push my legs until they ache. But I'm not stopping. The wind keeps whipping at me, blowing my hair in my face. It blows with all its force but I still keep going

I turn onto the river trail, running between the guide-post. I run past the houses with their long sloping lawns, bulleting down the path. I run, and my legs burn, and breathing feels like needle pricks in my lungs. Way ahead in the thick, wavy grass I spot two black and white things, probably rocks. I'm spent, exhausted, but I focus on that as my finish line, I'll make it to those rocks.

I get closer and can see those things aren't rocks. They're two geese hidden in the grass. I push my legs one last time until I've passed, then I slow to a walk, to a jog. Breathe. Breathe. Once, when we were fishing, Lyde told me about geese. He said that geese mate for life. His dad used to hunt geese but he gave it up after he shot a goose and found the mate just circling. Circling and honking at the other goose, like it was telling it to get up and get out of there. It wouldn't leave. It just kept circling.

Why do stupid geese know to stick together when people aren't even that smart? All of a sudden, I hate geese. "Go on. Go get out of here!" I yell. I pick up a fist-sized rock and hurl it with all my strength.

My rock falls short. Not even close. The geese don't jump or honk or rustle their feathers. They just turn and look at me, like they know exactly what they're doing and I don't even have a clue.

The Secret

"You didn't eat much tonight. Too many pine nuts in the pesto?"

"No."

"Too much olive oil?"

"No, Dad. It's fine. I'm just not feeling well." It's the understatement of the year. I'm tired and terrified and so queasy, like I rode an elevator up to the moon and then dropped back to earth.

"Is it the flu?"

"No, it's nothing." My stomach wobbles and churns.

Dad picks the glass pitcher up off the table. "Come out here and help me with this, will you?"

"With what?"

"Outside." I follow Dad to the sliding glass door. He passes me the pitcher and heaves, pushing on the door with both hands. "There's sand caught in the tracks. I'll have to get it cleaned it out."

He flips a switch in the carport and the lights flicker on. The piano sits in the corner, covered in a layer of dust. He takes the water from me and sets it on the ground, next to the piano.

"Aren't you ready to push it back inside?" I say.

"Maybe later," he says. Over by the piano, Dad gets down on his hands and knees. He reaches under the keyboard and yanks at a knob. The whole panel above the foot pedals comes loose, showing hundreds of copper and steel strings.

"Here, hold this." He stands up.

I hold onto the leaning panel, keeping it from dashing into pieces on the concrete floor, while Dad comes back with a blanket and spreads it out. Together, we carefully lay the panel on top. From the inside floor of the piano, he pulls out two huge water tumblers. "Hand me the water, will you?"

He fills the cups.

"You water the piano?" It's *loco*, crazy, insane. I chew my lip so I don't say any of those things.

"I need to, once a month. This dry air is awful on it."

We slide the panel back into place. I fold the blanket and press it into my stomach. My stomach that rolls and rumbles. My stomach that holds my secret.

Dad sits down at the piano and starts playing, while I slide into a chair. Tonight, it's not Simon and Garfunkle but some old sappy John Denver love songs.

I sink into the chair. *Take me home to the place I belong.* The song is so familiar it hurts. The words float around like her ghost. They used to love sitting side by side on the piano and singing these old songs. *The radio reminds me of my home far away.* What's Mom doing right now? Is she in her apartment missing us?

Dad presses hard on those piano keys, making those sad notes sing out louder, while the secret inside me grows.

I've collapsed on Bree's bed, exhausted, barely able to hold up the script. Bree spins the chair at her bedroom vanity around backwards and sits down. Just like with Marcus, I was too good of a tutor. I helped her get the part of the cowardly lion, and now we've got to memorize whole scenes from *The Wizard of Oz.*

While Bree studies her script, I close my eyes.

"Let's do page 40," she says. Then in a growly lion voice, "All right, I'll go in there for Dorothy. Wicked Witch or no Wicked Witch, guards or no guards…"

It sounds good, convincing even. She makes a great lion.

"Guard or no guards…"

"Hmm," I say.

"Mel, you missed your line."

"Sorry," I say, "I'm feeling all… *malo*." Bad, out of energy, exhausted, I'm feeling all of it.

"Maybe it's mono. It's been going around. You been kissing anyone new?"

I try to laugh but it comes out as a nervous grunt. "It's definitely not mono."

"The flu?"

"No." If only it were something that would fix itself after a few days of throwing up. I think about telling Bree the truth. What would she do? What would she say? She'd freak but then she'd help me figure everything out.

"One last scene, then let's take a break. On page 47, halfway down, where Dorothy says, 'Your majesty, if you were king you wouldn't be afraid of anything?'" She shakes her head in the most furious lion way. "Not nobody! Not no how!"

I'm on the page. It's my turn, my line. This is where I come in. I feel like an earthquake starting to rumble. A tornado starting to spin.

She holds up her fist. "Not nobody! Not no how!"

Maybe there's no stopping it. Maybe I have to tell her now. I start, "I…"

She drops her hand, and the playbook falls to the floor. "Mel, come on! What's going on?"

I breathe in, trying to fill my lungs with lion-like courage. "I need to tell you something."

"Okay?"

"Just don't freak out."

"Okay?" she says, her voice sounding wavy.

"I'm… well… there was that night at the dance." I study the floor, Snickers wrappers, hairspray, Sharpie, socks, hair tie. My heart slams away in my chest.

"Melina?" She squints at me, like she's trying to see me from far away.

And she is so far away. Bree with her perfect family that all march to church together. She's nothing like me. Nothing like my family, with Mom in Seattle and Dad here. No wonder she is squinting; we are far, far away, on different planets.

"Are you okay?"

"I mean… this is all wrong, don't you think? This play doesn't make any sense. I mean a lion, a tin man, and a scarecrow, what are they all supposed to be anyway? I mean it's bizarre. What is this play even about?"

She blinks. "It's *The Wizard of Oz.*"

"Well, it is kind of ridiculous, you know, with munchkins and yellow-brick roads and witches. There shouldn't be witches. It's terrifying. I mean, I don't think you should be putting this play on for kids. It'll freak them out."

Bree hurries over and put her hand on my forehead. "Maybe you have a fever." She turns to the door and yells, "Mamá!" She puts her hand on top of mine. "Maybe you are coming down with the flu. Something is definitely wrong."

And, of course, she's absolutely right.

136

Fishing

I don't know what else to do, so I drive. I follow the road out north of town, up what feels like Church Hill, because for some reason three different churches stand there in a row. When I get to the last one, to Lyde's church, I pull into the parking lot, the tires crunching on the loose gravel.

No one is around. The windows are dark. But the church sits there at the top of the slope with its steeple pointing up. I circle the parking lot and then stop and park. From here you can look out across the whole valley. See everyone's lights as they start to blink on.

I wait until the blue-black sky changes all the way to black and the stars come out one by one.

I haven't been here in a while. I even kind of miss Lyde's preacher who doesn't dress in a robe, who talks about love and forgiveness and doesn't go on and on about hell and damnation until he's spitting out the words. Lyde's preacher is kind of an everyday preacher, one whose sermons you can

137

stick in your back pocket and bring out whenever you need them. Not the kind that try to scare you into believing.

The preacher once said that God wants to talk to us. That prayer is like the best cell phone plan ever, with no fees and no cancellation. I prayed before, when I was little. Those were little-kid prayers, not the giant kind I need right now. I decide to try.

God, if you're there. And the jeans-wearing preacher says that you are and he seems like he wouldn't lie. And if anything that preacher is saying is true then…

I stop praying because right then the image of that pregnancy test pee stick comes to mind and I remember I prayed about that. I still can't believe.

Dang it, God! I'm really in the worst mess of my life. And why would you do that to me, God, just when I was trying to find you? I mean I was busy with stupid Marcus and I didn't come back to youth group but before then I was trying to find you. And it's like the whole huge carpet of the world has been ripped out from underneath me. And you have nothing to say about it.

And then I stop praying and I don't even add amen, because I don't think God is even there. I don't know if he is listening at all. And why would he do this to me? And if he listens and you plead and cry, and then he doesn't even help… what's the point of all that?

After school, I drive home and pull into the driveway. I can't do it. I can't go in and sit and just think anymore. I can't.

I shift into reverse and back out. Bree's at play practice, but maybe Lyde's home. Maybe his little brother will want to tell me knock-knock jokes again, and then we can all sit around watching cartoons and eating bowls of Frosted Flakes in front of the TV. Then maybe Lyde and I can go for a drive, and when we're all alone I can tell him. And then maybe, it will be like when I told him about Mom leaving, how he came over and sat by me at the pasta place in the booth. He put his arm around me and just stayed like that, even though his pasta got cold. Maybe it will be like that.

When I get to Lyde's house, his truck is gone. And I almost smack my head. How stupid: I know where he goes on Thursdays. I hit the gas and zoom away, following the signs to the Burbank highway, past the old railroad bridge. And sure enough, when I turn off and follow the dirt road east, there's the YO truck. I get out. Here along the river there's a muddy, earthy smell. I come around the bend, and there he is, standing in the middle of the river, waders hiked up to his chest, the sun shimmering around him. He's using his fly rod, casting, again and again, making his bait dance. It flies out and returns, smooth, effortless, like this is what he was born to do. He takes a step downstream and casts out again. I find a rock, sit, and the crickets hum around me.

I wait until he stops, grabs hold of his line and starts walking toward me, shuffling through the shallows of the river. "Melina?"

"Hey." I stand up.

He comes up the bank, puts one foot back, in a fencing stance and points his pole at me. "En garde," he says.

"Nice pants."

He moves his pole in a circle. "Not everyone can wear waders and look amazing."

"Very, very true," I say, feeling my mouth pull into a smile. It feels wonderful and odd. I don't know when the last time I smiled was.

"Are you going to join me?"

"I'm no good with the fly rod."

"I always carry a spinner too." We walk back to his truck and he pulls out a regular kind of fishing pole. "You remember how this works, right?"

I give him a shove. "Who caught the most last time?"

"That was just luck."

As we walk along the bank, the sun shines down, soft and warm, and I wonder if maybe this afternoon is so perfect, so good, that if I tell Lyde my not-so-good news everything will turn out okay. "You know, I haven't been that lucky lately."

"Hmm?"

I stop walking and face him. "I need to tell you something."

"Okay." He stops.

"It's about Marcus."

Lyde's lips go thin. He stands the fishing poles on the ground, all tight and rigid. "What about him?"

"There's just a mess. A big mess." Where do I even start? "I'm sorry I asked you to sneak me out to the dance."

Lyde shakes his head. "I should've said no."

"It was a mistake."

"He's not right for you. He never was."

I nod and it's like there's a river inside of me about to spill out and tell Lyde everything. "Like I said, I'm sorry…"

"But it's all over, right? It's not like you're seeing him anymore," he says, putting the fishing poles in one hand and squeezing my hand with the other. "I guess in the end, it doesn't really matter now, does it?"

I don't know what to say. But I stand there not telling him, because it feels too good, with Lyde's warm hand in mine. I stand there because I need to feel this. I need to feel that everything is going to be okay. His eyes shine at me, and I smile back. And for just that moment, everything is fine.

Sick

My stomach revolts against me like there's a war going on in there. Two sides are fighting, battling each other, heaving up on the one side, and then heaving up on the other. I stare at my laptop, trying to understand the sample SAT questions, but I'm so far behind I can't concentrate. My stomach lunges and lurches like it's possessed. I can't take anymore, and I stumble down the hall and into the bathroom. Quick-fast I shut the door and I'm there kneeling at the toilet and everything lunges out of me. I puke again and again and again until I'm empty.

Oh please, no more. But my stomach is a trooper. It's an extra-miler. It's a never-say-die-er. It tries, again and again, to throw up. I'm a puppet, a rag doll, just lunging and folding over, doing whatever my stupid stomach wants me to do.

When it's finally over, I scoot back, lean against the bathroom tub and hold my head in my hands.

"Melina?" Dad taps on the door. "Is everything okay? Are you all right?"

My stomach churns again, but it's empty. Please, it has to be empty. Go away, Dad. "Fine, Dad. I'm fine. I'll be out in a minute."

I reach over and twist on the bathtub faucet. The water pounds and splashes and hopefully drowns out my moaning. I lean over, lie all the way down on the pink bathroom mat, and close my eyes.

I wake to a splash of cold on my back. Water is pouring down the side of the tub! Quickly, I crank the faucet shut, plunge my hand into the tub, and release the drain stopper, soaking my arm. I jump up, grab the towels hanging on the towel bar and try to soak up the mess. I mop and clean. When the tub has drained, I haul the wet, drippy mess of towels and the bathmat into the tub, sit back against it, and cry.

When, finally, I decide I can probably make it back to my bed, I open the bathroom door and there's Dad, standing in the hall. His forehead is all wrinkled, and he stares at me, his arms crossed.

"Melina, we need to talk."

He knows.

"Let's go sit down."

We walk what seems like a green mile down the hall-way and into the living room. I sit on one couch and he sits on the other. Dad takes off his glasses and rubs his eyes. "I need you to be honest with me."

I nod but my heart thrums so fast, like a drumroll before walking the plank. "How long has this been going on?"

How long have I been pregnant? Is that what he means? I start counting back in my mind.

"Why didn't you talk to me about this?" Dad rubs and rubs his eyes like he doesn't want to see. He isn't ready for all of this, and neither am I.

How do you even say this out loud? It isn't something you can just say here in my living room, is it? I mean I haven't even told Bree yet.

"Melina, you're so smart. I never would have expected. I mean straight A's and well, I'm sorry, I should've been here with you and more understanding. But never in a million years would I guess…"

"Dad, fine. It's fine. Whatever. I mean I know. It was stupid. Just one stupid night. But it's over now. I can't believe it even happened."

"Listen, Melina. You can't tell me it's over now. I mean, I may have been kind of blind before, but I'm not going to believe it's over after I just heard you throwing up your breakfast in there. Eating disorders are a serious problem; you can't just turn it on and off like a switch."

"Wait… Eating disorder?" I stare at him. "You think I have an eating disorder?"

Dad puts his glasses on. "I never see you eating anymore and then when you finally do, you go into the bathroom and throw it up."

This is no time to laugh but still, I crack up. "Dad, I don't have an eating disorder."

"Then what is it? What in the world are we talking about?"

I feel it in the air. The world stops spinning on its axis because it's finally, finally time to tell. I take a breath and the words fall out. "I'm pregnant."

He sits there still as a statue. He shakes his head. He doesn't believe me.

"Dad, I'm sorry. I promise. It's true."

Then he stares at me, like he's so confused he doesn't even know my name anymore.

Carnitas

I decide to tell Bree during lunch. As she drives down the road, I'm about to start, to say something like, *well you'll never guess…* but then I figure maybe I should wait until we've eaten. Maybe it's better to freak someone out if they've got a full stomach.

We go to where the *La Familia* Taco Truck is parked, order, and come back to the car, our paper plates filled with the best tacos in town. But as we sit and Bree unwraps her *carnitas*, suddenly, it's too much. The spices and onions and peppers, the smell of it all swirls and my stomach swirls with them. It's cold outside, but I have to roll down the window and breathe in the non-taco-scented air.

"You okay?" asks Bree.

I stare at the pool of grease on her plate. "No, I'm not."

"Sick again?"

I blow out a breath.

"Really, Melina you've got to see a doctor. What if it's, like, cancer?"

"It's not cancer," I say to her paper plate.

"But it could be, I mean. You've been sick a lot."

"Bree, holy crap, it's not cancer."

"You can't be sure."

"I am sure because… I'm pregnant."

"Ha!" She laughs and a tiny piece of taco meat flies out of her mouth. And it makes me smile. And she laughs a little more. "Yeah, right. You're pregnant… and we're taking our rendition of *The Wizard of Oz* to Broadway."

I stop with the smile, give her a no-joke look. "Bree, I'm serious."

"Stop already," she says, still grinning.

I don't move. "It's true. It happened the night of the Harvest Dance. I didn't tell you because I didn't plan on it. None of it was supposed to happen, and now this…"

Silence.

I don't know where to look. I stare down at my flimsy paper plate, at a cast-off penny on the floor, at my worn-down, falling-apart sneakers. And then back up at Bree.

She gives me this look, like I'm not the same girl she walked to 7-Eleven with all through junior high. Like we didn't search my couch cushions for quarters to buy Slurpees. And, Slurpees in hand, I didn't sit there on the curb outside the store, with loose gravel under my sneakers,

147

and Bree didn't stand up to do her impressions of Ms. Mason, putting her hands on her hips and saying, "Now people." And we didn't laugh until our mouths flew open, and she didn't point at my purple Slurpee-stained tongue and I didn't point to her blueberry lips and we didn't laugh even harder. She looks at me as if none of that happened. Ever.

She reaches over and hugs me and she still doesn't say anything because, sure, she doesn't know what to say.

When we pull away, I sit back. "I don't think I can ever eat *carnitas* again."

She keeps her hand on my arm. "Well," she says at last, and why is she looking at my arm and not at me, why? "My cousin Mari Carmen did okay, you know."

Her words swirl around me. "My *tia* threw a fit. But you know… it's okay… not perfect. But… he's the cutest kid, Melina, I swear. Adorable little basketball shoes. The boyfriend's… a *todo payaso*, but even so… know what I mean?"

But there's an undercurrent to her words. A removal that wasn't there before. She's still her, but I'm not still me. Not the me she thought I was. She keeps talking, her words a low buzz in my ears. I can hardly hear her. All I can do is wonder if we will ever laugh over purple- and blue-colored tongues again.

Planning

Later, when my mind stops swirling around as much as my stomach, I realize I need a better job, with more hours and better pay. My sneakers, jeans, backpack, everything is wearing out. I need stuff and I guess a baby will, too. Cleaning the office at Best Life Realty twice a week isn't enough money.

I call up Bree. "What does your cousin do for work?"

"Which one? I have a gazillion."

"The one with the baby, what does she do?"

"Oh, Mari Carmen. She's a receptionist. And she takes college classes at night, when her mom takes the baby." I rock up onto my toes. That could work, couldn't it? I could answer phones at an office, and a baby could sit around in one of those carrier things. And then I could get those college classes done, too. And then maybe after I figure things out, I could get to Portland State University. Maybe I could work everything out. I pick up my laptop and start searching for jobs. And once I've got a long list, I start calling.

"Do you have two years of experience?"

"Do you have any post-high-school education?"

"Are you able to work full-time?"

"No," I answer over and over. I keep searching and calling and trying for two full days. But every time, the answer is no.

I'm on my bed, ready for a Saturday afternoon nap, when I hear Dad's phone ring, and I freeze.

"Mel," he calls.

I jump off the bed and start digging around. I find one shoe and yank it on.

"Mel," says Dad louder.

Frantically, I dig under my bed and search, pushing away a cereal bowl, two water bottles, a study notebook. There's the shoe, under my sweatshirt. I stretch, grabbing it with my fingertips, and yank it on. Stumbling, I bolt out of my room and down the hall. But there's Dad, waiting at the front door like a police officer with a warrant for my arrest.

"I need some air."

He crosses his arms. "No more."

"Dad, I swear I'm feeling sick."

He holds out his phone. "Talk to her."

But I can't. I can't say those words again. Telling Dad and telling Bree, it's been too much, I can't do it anymore.

"Melina, please." His shoulders sag and his eyes are bloodshot.

"Okay... okay," I say, taking his phone, and we both walk into the kitchen. Dad loops an apron over his neck, and I sit down on a barstool. "Hey."

"Melina," says Mom, stretching out my name like it's a Band-Aid.

She knows. I can tell from the sound of her voice. She knows.

I look over at Dad, who's yanking out a mixing bowl from the cupboard, clanging it on the countertop. I want to run over and throw my arms around him, hug him for not making me tell her.

"How are you?" And I sit there, just listening to her voice. It's the voice she used when I was little, when I came to her with scraped-up knees or slivers in my hands. "I don't want you to worry. I've got this. I have the name of a doctor and we'll get you all fixed up."

Fixed up?

"I can fly in and we'll get everything over within just a few hours."

"You'll fly here?"

"I don't want you to worry."

I feel all airy and light, and suddenly, I want to lie down and rest. I go into the living room and lie down on the rug.

"Melina, hon, are you there?"

"Yeah," I say.

"Really, it's a simple procedure, and I'll be there every step of the way."

"You'll come home?"

"Sure. Everything can be fixed," she says.

She can fix it? Can everything be tied up, nice and neat like the stories she used to read me when I was little? Like the man in the yellow hat, who fixes all of Curious George's messes?

I don't know. I don't know. I don't know. But what I say is, "Okay."

Maybe

Bree lounges on our couch with a bag of pretzels as I open the drawer in the entertainment center and search our DVDs. "Comedy, action, drama, horror?"

"How about *The Wizard of Oz*?"

I fling a pillow right at her face. With a rare showing of a sports-like reflex, she grabs it out of the air. "No musicals," I say.

"Well, no sappy ones. Nothing where anyone has a terminal illness, a life-altering car accident, or where the dog dies."

"Fair enough." I flip through Mom's documentaries, mixed with Dad's cooking shows. "Well… my mom's coming back."

"*Híjole,*" she says.

"Just for a visit. But maybe she'll decide to stay."

"Did she say that?"

"It could happen."

"She'll probably be here a lot more, you know, helping get ready for the baby."

I flip faster through the DVDs. "Maybe."

"She'll help, won't she? Get baby clothes and diapers and stuff?"

"I don't think so." All our movies are in a giant scrambled mess. "She says she's coming to fix it."

"What do you mean?"

I take breath. "She wants me to go to the doctor—to take care of everything."

Bree sits up, and the pretzel bag makes a sharp crinkle noise. "Wait a second." She's shaking her head. "You don't mean an abortion."

Abort. Stop. Cease. Desist. Yes, I want all this craziness to stop. I want to get off this awful roller coaster.

"*Híjole,* Melina, you can't do that." She keeps shaking her head like she's in a nightmare and she can't wake up.

"Easy for you to say," I say.

"What?"

A ball of heat forms in my gut and rushes through me. "It's easy to tell others what to do, isn't it? But it's not you and not your body. It's not your mom who's taken off and your dad who pounds on the piano at night and not you getting used and then tossed aside by some dude who thinks high school is 'casual' now, is it?"

"But, geez Mel, it's a life. You'd be taking a life."

Now I'm the one shaking my head because I don't know. "Is it? What if it's just a bunch of cells, dividing and multiplying?"

"Of course, it is," says Bree.

I stare down into the giant mess of movies and I still don't know.

As soon as the school bell rings, I hurry down the stairs, not stopping at my locker, not grabbing my jacket. I'll find Marcus and maybe we can go to a quiet place, I'll tell him, and we'll figure out what to do. Maybe he'll want to be a part of everything. Maybe we can even become a team again and work together just like before.

I wait at the bottom of the stairs, next to the case full of school trophies. In the case, there's an empty spot, one ready and waiting for a trophy. It is time for a win, isn't it? Time for something good. Time for something shiny and bright that you can lift up on your shoulders and cheer about. People pour out of the hallway and come tromping down the stairs, rushing out.

Here comes Marcus, with his gang of friends.

"Hey, Marcus," I call out.

He glances over but then keeps talking with Tyrell.

"Marcus!" I say louder, and I push through the crowd until I'm walking next to him.

155

"Oh, hi, Melina," he says like he didn't see or hear me before. Frank and Tyrell keep moving with the crowd, pushing towards the doors.

"We need to talk," I say as we're stopped there, right in the middle of the giant stream of people.

He looks up and blows out a breath. "This isn't a good idea."

I clutch my books tighter. "It's really important. We need to go somewhere."

He chews his lip. "Not now. I've got a meeting with my recruiter. Then I've got a full day of farm work." He looks back up the stairs. "And Kensly won't like it."

"You don't…," I start but before I finish, he's moving again, like he's trying to blast off, far away.

"I can't right now. I'm sorry." He takes off running, before we can even get to maybe.

Suitcase

The automatic doors behind us open and cold air blows in. People dodge around Dad and me as we stand in silence. It's been four—four—months without Uno games, without barbeques, without us all together as a family.

She comes strolling down the hall, her coat folded over her arm. When she sees us, she hurries over. She grabs me by the shoulders and looks me up and down. "Melina," she says, almost in a gasp, and quick-fast she wraps me up in a hug.

I don't move. I stay there, stiff as a board. Because blast it! Why did she do this to us? I stay there as unfeeling as a lamppost. And I close my eyes and try not to move, but then I can't help it. I hug her back, just a little.

She steps back, keeping hold of my arms. "Honey, I wish you would've come to see me in Seattle. I think you've grown."

"It's too hard to miss school," I lie.

Dad steps closer. "Annette, good to see you."

She nods. "Hello, Paul."

"How was your flight?" he asks.

"Uneventful."

Standing between them feels so natural, the way it should be. I wish I were little again, to be wearing a sundress and saltwater sandals, to slide each of my hands into theirs, and walk off, the three of us links in a construction-paper chain.

"Can I give you a hand?" Dad reaches out for her carry-on bag.

"No, I've got it."

"Please, let me help," he says.

We stay there with a whole crowd veering around. "Really, Paul. I've got it." She checks her watch. "But we need to get going." She starts over to the car rental counter.

"Wait, Annette." Dad drums his fingers on his leg, like he's playing piano scales. "Why don't you use my car?"

"I planned on getting a rental."

"It'll save you time, with no lines and an easy return. I can drive Melina's car if I need to go anywhere."

I can't imagine Dad taking his clients around in my little Chevy, with the passenger's window that doesn't roll down and the heater that only works if you bang on it three times. But I say, "Sure, that would work great."

"I need to check the clutch anyway," he says, nodding.

Mom looks at the car rental line. "Maybe just this once." And together, the three of us walk out the airport doors. When we step outside, the wind whips around us.

"Wait," I say, running back and opening the automatic doors. "Hold on. We forgot. We didn't get your suitcases."

Mom looks at me all squinty. "I didn't bring any other suitcases."

I glance over at her tiny suitcase and my breath sticks inside me, aching. She's supposed to have suitcases. Lots of big suitcases stuffed full of dresses and skirts and shoes and jackets. Not a little one that hardly holds a hairdryer.

We get in Dad's car and drive away in silence. Outside, the wind is turning the day into a hazy mess. This isn't the way it's supposed to be, none of it. I sit back and press my hands together. "How long are you going to be here?"

She looks over at Dad, who is driving extra slow. "Well, I've planned on being here for your initial recovery and then your dad will take over after that."

I press my hands harder. "How long?"

Mom turns her bracelet in a circle. "The procedure is relatively simple. It shouldn't take you long to feel better."

"Who's hungry? We could stop and get something to eat," says Dad.

"No," says Mom sharply. She pivots around. "You haven't had anything to eat or drink, have you?"

I shake my head and press my hand against the cold window.

"Good." She turns back. "Melina can't eat before the procedure."

My empty stomach churns, and my throat feels scratchy.

"We can later, after everything's done. But nothing, not a drop, before."

Dad drives the long way home. Going down Court Street and through the city, instead of circling out by the wheat fields and the new subdivision. "The marquee at McDonald's blew down in a big windstorm," he says, pointing to the empty pole. "And Albertsons is open all night now."

Mom pulls off her gloves and rests her head back.

The wind blows hard, rattling the windshield wipers. "At Mark Twain Elementary, they had to add portable classrooms." When he pulls into our driveway, he stops several feet outside the carport.

Mom sits up. "Is that the piano? Why in the world is the piano in the carport?"

Silence.

The car is stifling. I crack open the window. "We just barely moved it out. Just a few days ago." I lie again. Suddenly, I've turned into the world's greatest liar.

"But why?"

"For a change. For something different," I say.

"It should be brought inside," she says.

Dad stares straight ahead. "Why don't you come inside?"

"I could go check into the hotel. We have three hours, but I want to get there early."

"Just come in for a few minutes," he says.

She nods.

I get out of the car, away from her too-little suitcase, and slam the door. At the front door, Dad turns the key, pushes the door open and moves aside. Mom hesitates but then steps through with a big stride. Inside, she sits on one edge of the couch, like she's a visitor or something.

"Annette, I would offer you something to drink but…," he says, looking over at me.

"I know. I get it. Nothing for me," I say.

He moves forward, his hands on his knees, as if he's working a real estate deal.

Mom smooths out her skirt. "Melina, I don't want you to worry about a thing. I'll be at your side every step of the way."

Dad takes off his glasses and rubs his eyes. "I guess… I mean I guess this is what you need to do. We've talked about it. You're so young… there's no other option."

Mom nods. "Your dad and I are together on this."

They are together, but only for a few hours.

Dad puts his glasses in his pocket. "It has to be the right thing for Melina. What do you want, Melina? Is this what you want?"

What do I want? I want them back together. I want us all in this house together. I want him playing the piano inside where it should be and her sitting next to him, leaning her head on his shoulder. That's what I want.

But instead, I got this. I look down at my stomach. "I don't know," I say, the words choking out. "I didn't mean… It shouldn't have… And now… I just don't know."

"You shouldn't have left," Dad whispers, staring at Mom's shoes.

Mom straightens up on the couch. "Have you told Melina the reason behind our separation?"

I shake my head and press my hands into the couch. No, this isn't the time. They can't fight now.

"Did you tell her about your so-called client? Does she know about her?"

No one moves. Not a sound. The wind stops howling. I can't breathe. Mom's words float out there and then they sink in.

Dad falls back in the chair, like he was shoved. His voice is a whisper. "You were gone all the time. Working for days and weeks on end. And when you came home you weren't even here."

I shake my head. A hundred times I shake my head. I have to get out and get away from them. I stand up. I walk into the kitchen and out the back door. Away. Onto the patio. Behind me, they yell. Sharp words. I walk out into the haze. The wind pelts me with sand and dust. I keep going out into the yard. Screaming. I'm screaming. I'm yelling at the wind, which howls right along with me.

7-Eleven

I keep walking, harder and faster, until the asphalt blurs under me. I walk until the wind whips my hair and my skin is covered with a layer of sand. All of those fights, I didn't understand. I heard them fighting and I didn't get it. Those nights, I'd sneak out of the house and jog around the neighborhood jealous of all the homes without anyone yelling.

Dad. My dad. The one who always makes chocolate-chip pancakes for me on the first day of school. The one who plays the piano with his whole heart. The one who checks the oil in my car and replaces the battery cables. He cheated… on Mom… on us. I keep walking. Fine. Mom can yell at him all afternoon and all night and then longer.

Fine. I'll stay at school, the library, and clear away from their mess. I don't need to go home. I keep walking, passing Lyde's house and all the way down the next road, passing Bree's. They're in class right now, just like Marcus, who doesn't even know that I'm pregnant. What would he say? Would he be okay with me going to the doctor? He'd probably want me to, wouldn't he?

Just like Mom and Dad, we're in a mess. But it wasn't always a mess. They came together and made me and I'm proof, aren't I, of something more? And as a family aren't we more than just our separate selves? We have proof, there in the house. Stacks and stacks of photo albums. Photos from San Diego with our sunburned noses. Photos of carnivals and cotton candy. And a closetful of games, Uno and Sorry and Monopoly. Even though right now, Dad and Mom are a mess, we weren't always like that.

And maybe Marcus and I won't always be a mess. We came together and created something that is more than just us. Is it this something's fault that we made it? Is it this something's fault that I don't know what to do? How can I go to the doctor and climb on some operating table and stop this something from coming?

I keep walking until I stand across the street from 7-Eleven. My throat aches with dryness and my body aches from I don't know what. Cars zoom back and forth and when the road is quiet, I hurry across. I march into the store and go straight to the Slurpee machine. I grab the biggest, jumboest-sized cup, put it under the purple swirling window, and pull the lever.

Giant Slurpee in hand, I go over to the cashier and

count out my change. I have more than enough, much more. I walk out and take a long swig from that drink and it soothes my aching throat.

The wind dies down and I use my sleeve to wipe grit off my face. I walk home with the sun shining on my back. I drink my Slurpee and walk. When I get home, my car is gone and there's Mom looking out the window. As I come up the sidewalk, she runs out and wraps me in a hug. With my face in her hair, I say, "I'm not doing it."

"Let's go inside," she whispers.

Once inside, she points to the Slurpee cup. "Did you drink that?" Her lips press into a line. "I must've told you a dozen times, you can't eat or drink anything."

"I'm not going to do it."

"Melina, honey, I'm sorry. But I can't possibly reschedule. I have so many clients depending on me. And, besides, time is up. We can't wait any longer."

I stand up straight. I've grown some since she left, and now my eyes are level with hers. "I'm not doing it today. I'm not doing it tomorrow. I'm not doing it next week. I'm going to have this baby."

"Melina," she says softly, putting her hand on my arm, but I don't want it there.

I shrug her off and walk away.

SPRING

Telling

Later that night, I call Bree but her mom picks up. "Melina?"

"*Soy yo*," I say, practicing.

"*Un momento, mi vida.*" I smile at the—*mi vida*. She's always calling me things like that—my life, my treasure, my soul. What's she going to call me when she finds out I'm pregnant? My *estúpido*? In the background, I hear her mom call, "Brianna!" Then there's more noise: the boys yelling, some banging and thumping.

"Mel?" says Bree.

"Hey," I say.

"Sorry, I lost my phone again. Hold on." A door slams. "*Holiness*, Melina, I've been thinking about you all day. You okay?"

"I wanted to tell you…" I stare down at my stomach, wondering how big it will get. "I didn't do it."

"What do you mean?"

169

"My mom got here. She brought this really small suitcase. She's only planning on staying overnight and then I found out…" It's too much. I can't tell her everything. "Well, my parents got into this giant fight, and, well, I told her no."

"*Híjole*, are you serious?"

"Yeah."

"When are you?"

"I'm not going to, ever. I'm having this baby."

"What made you change your mind?"

"I don't think I changed it. I just finally know for sure."

Out in the field next to the school someone left an old, weathered soccer ball. I kick it against the fence. *Clang.* The chain links rattle. I kick it again. *Clang.* I keep kicking, slamming the ball again and again.

I've been trying to talk to Marcus all week. It was going to be yesterday for sure, but after school, when I saw him, he had his arm around Kensly, and no way was I going to tell him with her around.

I slam the ball again. He needs to know. Bree says the father of her cousin's baby doesn't do anything. But Marcus can't be like that. He'll have to step up.

I kick again but the ball rolls, bounces off the fence post, and rolls out into the parking lot. As I jog over and pick it up, I see Marcus walking towards his car. My heart pounds with every step as I sprint over. A car passes by, its stereo blaring.

"Hey," I call.

When Marcus sees me, he scans the parking lot like he's looking for an escape route. "Hey," he says, as I catch up to him.

I hold that soccer ball tight. "There's something…"

"Sorry, Melina. I should go. I've got to get to the farm, move some irrigation pipes."

I shake my head. "We need to talk."

He stares at the soccer ball. "I can't… It's Kensly. She gets really jealous."

The ball, I want to slam it at him and make him listen. My heart pounds in my throat. "I don't care about Kensly, all right? Just listen—I'm pregnant."

He stands still as a statue.

"It's true."

"No."

I nod. And for a second, I'm glad I wasn't the only one, with crazy eyes, shaking my head in disbelief. And I'm glad I wasn't the only one who can't believe it. And I'm glad I wasn't the only one who stands there in shock as if they've just been told a meteor is hurtling toward earth and we're all going to die.

"No, you're not."

"Marcus…"

"How?"

I give him a you-are-an-idiot look.

"It can't be." He takes a few steps backward.

"Wait…"

"You're lying." He turns and runs. He keeps running toward his car.

And I stand there, planted solid, gripping the ball so tight my fingers turn white.

Job Hunting

Maybe until I can find a nice office job, I can work at the mall. There are so many stores out there, all probably hiring. I grab my keys and drive out.

Hours later, my feet ache, I'm sweaty and tired, and waiting in line at Just Juice. Barb's Dress Shop doesn't hire anyone still in high school. Rings and Things needs someone for the morning. And at J. J. Morales, the manager took my résumé, mashed it into a bulging folder and said, "I have too many employees already." All of those and another bunch of stores gave me a heaping truckload of NO.

At Just Juice, the girl working the register wears a tower of fake fruit on her head. Each time she moves, the miniature pineapple wobbles like it's about to fall off.

"Special of the day—pineapple smoothie," says the girl, popping her gum.

"Not pineapple," I say, feeling my stomach surge. "Just a plain orange juice." I hand her my money, and a plastic lime drops from her hat into the register. She plucks it from the change drawer and tosses it in the garbage.

"Idiot manager," she says, rolling her eyes. "Ridiculous costume."

I shrug. "But it's a job."

"A rotten job."

"Are you hiring?"

"Really?" Her eyebrows shoot up. "You want to work here?" She points at her head. "You can see this, right?"

"I really need a job."

"Weekends are crazy. Can you work then?"

"Sure, and any time after school."

She nods and goes to get my drink.

Blending fruit, talking to customers, I could work here. Maybe we'd get to try new recipes, blend different things together.

She returns with my juice. "Joe does the hiring. He should be back in half an hour. Come back then and I'll tell him about you."

"Great." And as I walk out, I want to jump up and kiss the big orange in the sign up there.

Everything starts falling into place. Joe wants me to start work on Monday, and I already have a work week lined up. And when he brings out a pile of uniforms, I remember and pick one size bigger. I don't know what I'll do about all my homework, but maybe some shifts will be slow and I can do it here.

When I get home, I celebrate by sinking into the stuffed couch with a bag of potato chips, a tub of ranch dip, and the remote. I'm still clicking through shows, trying to find something good, when the front door creaks open.

"Hey kiddo," says Dad. He comes in carrying a take-out box.

"Hi," I say, sinking down further in the couch. Ever since Mom's visit, we've been walking around in our own separate bubbles. Now he crosses in front of the TV and sits down on the other couch.

"I brought you home some spinach salad. It's filled with protein and lots of iron."

"Okay."

"Did you decide on a doctor?"

"I'm narrowing it down." After Mom got back to Seattle, she emailed me a list of the doctors who accept our health insurance. She wants me to use the one I've been seeing since I was a kid. But I'm not going to an old guy who can't even take care of the hair growing in his ears.

"I can call and make you an appointment."

"I've got it," I say, figuring I could wait a while. My stomach isn't even sticking out yet.

"Also, I want to meet with Marcus and his mom as soon as possible."

"I know. This week is really busy. I'll have to do it next week," I say. I pop a chip in my mouth and stare at the TV, hoping he'll go away.

"You know, you shouldn't eat only chips."

"There are a lot of things people do that they shouldn't."

He doesn't say anything.

My phone rings and I jump up, thrilled to have an excuse to leave. Behind me, the floor creaks as Dad walks off. "Hello?"

"Melina?"

I thought Marcus would call but not for a few more days. "Yeah."

"We need to talk."

"I know."

"That was a pretty rotten joke."

"What?"

"The thing you said the other day. I mean it's not funny."

I shake my head. "Marcus, you don't get it."

"You're messing with me."

"It's true."

"I'm not going to stop seeing Kensly."

"I don't care about Kensly."

"Aren't you on the pill?"

"What? Why? Why would you say that?"

176

"That's what… girls do."

I pick up the giant physics book on my desk and wish I could throw it at him.

"Are you even sure it's mine?"

I clamp my teeth together. Hate. Red-hot hate. I hate him.

"And if you are, then you should go take care of it."

"I won't… I'm not doing that." I wait and then say, "Besides, it's too late."

Nothing. Then:

"You can't do this to me. I'm going into the Air Force. There's nothing you can do to make me stay. Leave me alone already."

I click off the phone. "Idiot." I say, and throw it on the bed. Fine. Go. Get out of here. *Make him stay?* He can leave today. Go on to boot camp already. Get screamed at and run drills until he drops in a heap to the ground.

Two Jobs

Two days later, I'm surrounded by sickeningly sweet smells. My stomach churns and I keep feeling lightheaded. I measure out the frozen fruit and juice and dump it into the blender. The high-screaming whirl makes my head ache. The hands on the banana clock hardly move, and after this, I still have to go clean the office.

When the smoothie is ready, I pour it into a cup but a fruit glob slips, making everything splatter. Quickly, I wipe everything down with a towel, snap on the lid, and take it over to the customer. "Here you go, one Mango Madness."

The lady starts to walk away. Then she flips around, dropping the drink on the counter. "Excuse me," she says loudly, shaking drips from her hands and yanking out napkins. "This cup is filthy."

Joe walks over and snatches it up. "Sorry," he says, nodding over at where I'm wiping off the counter. "She's in training." He tosses the cup into the garbage. "I'll create you a new drink."

"Sorry," I say, straightening the fruit hat on my head.

"How hard is it to serve a clean cup?" she asks, still dabbing at her hands.

How hard is it to be a decent human being? I've got splotches of juice everywhere. How was I supposed to know the cup wasn't squeaky clean?

Joe shouts over the grind of the blender. "Melina, can you sweep the floor?"

I walk away, wadding the corner of my apron up in my hand. Later, after a lecture from Joe about *pristine presentation*, I finally drive off toward the real-estate office, wishing I could go home and climb into bed. On the seat beside me sits the fruit hat. The grapes droop, the orange keeps popping off, and the strawberries have already lost their shine.

Doctor

The next night after work, I plop down at the kitchen table and drag out my chemistry textbook. Outside, Dad plays the piano. It's a Beethoven sonata that starts with a flowing melody but as he plays, it turns into a thunderstorm song with pounding runs and fierce banging chords.

When the music stops, Dad comes inside and sits across from me. He takes off his fogged-up glasses, cups his hands together, and blows into his red fingers.

"Isn't it too cold to be outside?"

"I suppose."

"Don't you think you should move the piano inside?"

"I will sometime."

I shake my head. Confusion. That's all I am, confusion.

"Do you have a lot of homework tonight?" he asks.

"A couple of hours."

"With that new job and all your homework, how are you going to get the rest you need?"

I shrug. "I need the money."

Dad puts his glasses back on. "Maybe my business will pick up."

I've seen him up at night, hunched over a pile of bills. Homes aren't selling right now, and Mom keeps complaining about the high cost of everything in Seattle and the law firm's low pay.

"Tomorrow we're going to your doctor's appointment, right?"

"Sure, sure."

"No more stalling."

I scratch at a dried splatter of orange smoothie on my arm. Three pages of chemistry to finish and I'm still covered in splatters. I don't care about going to the stupid doctor. All I want right now is to finish my homework, take a shower, and go to sleep.

***

When I get to the doctor's office, a nurse takes me into a small exam room. "Take a seat and relax. The doctor will be with you in a minute."

I nod at the table with that crinkly paper. "Do I have to sit up there?"

"No, you can wait in the chair," she says on her way out.

On the wall is a giant diagram of a baby growing inside of a stomach with all the organs labeled just like in biology class. The baby looks huge, like it's squishing everything and taking over the girl's body and there's nothing she can do about it. I pick up a magazine and flip through, but I keep staring at that giant baby on the wall.

After a quick knock, in walks a lady with blond strands pulling out from a messy ponytail. "I'm Doctor Nelleson, and you must be Melina."

I roll up that magazine into a cylinder, so it's like a running baton.

"How have you been feeling?"

"Fine. I guess."

She sits on the round spinning chair, puts her laptop on the counter and scrolls around. "Your medical history looks good. Any problems from your past ankle injury?"

"It's okay now." Good enough that I could run straight out of here.

"Have you felt the baby move?"

I nod.

She talks about pregnancy symptoms I hope won't happen, like swollen ankles and stretch marks and heartburn. She talks for so long I start wondering about her other patients. Doesn't she have other people she needs to scare?

"Climb up on the table and I will measure your stomach."

"In my regular clothes?" I ask.

"For now."

She stretches a measuring tape from a little bit above my bellybutton to way below my gut. "The measurement coincides with the dates you've given, looks like you're about four, almost five months along. You should've been in much, much sooner."

"I don't like…" I'm about to say doctors but I catch myself. I wave my hand around. "You know, all this stuff." I motion at the countertop filled with tongue depressors, cotton balls, and giant Q-tips. Just looking at them makes my throat ache.

"We'll take some blood and do some lab work. You must come in every month without fail. Okay? So we can keep you and your baby healthy."

I nod.

"And will we be seeing the baby's father at any of these visits?"

"Hardly," I say and it comes out like a snort.

Her eyes stay on me awhile. She takes a card out of her pocket. "Between visits, if you have questions about anything, call the office." I reach for the card, but she pulls it back.

"Sorry, one moment." She pulls a pen from her pocket, and using the exam table, she writes something on the back of the card. "If you have questions or any problems not during office hours, you can call my cell." She writes the numbers in big, solid print that you can't mistake or mess up. "And Melina, why don't you call me Dr. Kate," she says, as she opens the door and calls for the nurse.

Click

After school, I slide into the driver's seat and dig through my backpack. Phone, calculator, gum. Where are my keys? I can't be late for work. Yesterday, Cassandra clocked in three minutes late and Joe lectured both of us on the *importance of punctuality.* There, finally, I find my key, put it in the ignition, and turn.

Click.

I try again.

Click. Click. Nothing. No engine sputtering. No revving. I slam my fist on the steering wheel. Come on. All around me cars are taking off. I keep trying. *Click.*

I'm about to try the key again, but the passenger door opens, Marcus slips inside and sits down. He stares at me— well, at my stomach.

"What?"

"That's what I want to know, Melina. What are you doing?"

"I'm trying to drive to work."

"If this is about money, I don't have any. Not a cent. The farm is my grandpa's. He's just letting us live there."

"Money? How can this be about money?"

He shifts around. "Then what? Is it about Kensly? You're mad at me because of her? I mean… We've been together on and off for years. And when she saw us together, that flipped her out and… I'm sorry. I didn't mean for…"

"This isn't about Kensly or money or anything. This"— I look down at my stomach—"just is."

"You're ruining my life," he says. He opens the door, gets out and shuts it with a slam.

Idiot.

I turn the key again. *Click.*

Mom calls after that first doctor visit, to make sure I actually went. I did, but not the exact day she wanted and to a different doctor than she recommended. This is my decision and I'm going to do it my way.

One month later, after my second doctor visit, she calls again. "How was the doctor visit?" she asks.

I open the fridge. Behind the pickles, in a far corner, there's a container of ravioli. I open it up and take a whiff. It smells fine but it's not worth the risk. "Same as before."

"What about your blood tests?"

"They're fine."

"Your PH levels?"

"I don't know."

"Your iron level?"

I pick up a container of mashed potatoes. "I think it's okay."

"Did the doctor mention any problems or concerns?"

"Mom, everything is fine, all normal." I return the potatoes and get some carrots instead. Doctor Kate said I need to gain more weight, but my stomach already sticks out so much it's getting hard to hide.

As I walk into school, I stretch my sweatshirt out over my stomach. If I only wear sweatshirts from now on, maybe no one will know. I turn down the hall and there's Bree, hanging out by my locker.

I spin the dial around, searching for the right number. She puts her hand on my arm, and immediately I know something's wrong.

"What's going on?" I ask, as I slip off my backpack. Suddenly it seems so heavy, more than I can handle.

She holds open my backpack while I empty it, shoving books into my locker. "I heard some things," she says, her voice low.

I shove the last book in, terrified of what she's about to say. "What things?"

"I guess this morning Marcus started saying stuff."

"Saying what?"

"Stupid stuff. He's a *tonto gigante,* a giant idiot." The warning bell rings and Bree links her arm through mine and walks me down the hall.

"What is he saying?" I ask again.

"Really, he's just full of lies. I think our best plan is to ignore him," she says. At the end of the hall, she turns to go. "I've gotta run, but let's go to *El Mercado* for lunch okay? My treat." She gives my arm a squeeze and steps away.

"What lies?" I ask, but she's already gone.

As I walk down the hall, the baggy sweatshirt I bought at Fred Meyer, men's size medium, suddenly seems too small. I yank on the front, trying to make it bigger. Around me, I can feel others watching me and suddenly, their voices start to buzz.

"Not his fault."

"Tricked him."

"Planned the whole thing."

I shake my head. More voices, like the buzz of a thousand killer bees.

"She's desperate."

"Won't let him go."

A line of sweat drips down my back. But… if they all

187

know… If word spread through the school like a brush fire… then Lyde…

Please, no! I rush to his locker but he isn't there. Ahead of me, in the crowd of jackets, there is his army-green coat. I follow him, like a stalker. He slams open the door to the stairwell and runs down. As I hurry to catch up, he jumps the last few stairs and bullets out the school lobby. I reach the last stair just as he shoves the outside door so hard it rattles and shakes.

Once we're outside, I yell, "Lyde!"

He slows and turns, his hands in fists. "Melina?" he says, like my name is a question.

"Wait."

He finally stops, halfway to his car.

"Melina?" he says again, looking at me in unbelief.

"There's something I need to tell you," I say.

"Is it true?" His face clenches, like the air smells rotten. His eyes fall to my stomach.

I look to the ground, to the old, torn-up asphalt that someone needs to patch up and fix. What's wrong with people? Why isn't anyone coming to fix this parking lot?

"Is it?" he asks again.

"No, I don't know what you heard but it's not true." But this is Lyde, my friend; I can't lie. "But…," my voice squeaks, "some of it is."

"You were with him?" He shakes his head.

I nod.

"He treated you like crap."

"I know."

He closes his eyes. "You were with someone who doesn't even know you? Who doesn't love you."

"Love?" I choke out a painful laugh. "What even is that? How do you love someone and then pack up and move away?"

He puts out his hands, like he's trying to show me something. "Mel, you don't get it, do you? You can't see." He shakes his head and his face turns to stone.

And I take off running before he can leave me too.

Baby Clothes

Outside, spring is supposed to be bursting and blooming but everything is still gray and dull and cold. The only thing growing is my stomach. I pull on my sweats, sliding them down so that the waistband sits below my bulging stomach.

I go to the kitchen table and place my homework in three piles: late, very late, and getting a D or an F late. My dream of Portland State University now seems like it belonged to someone else. I hear a quick knock and the door squeaks open. "¿*Oye*, Melina?"

"In here," I yell. Bree comes in carrying two huge shopping bags and heaves them onto the table.

"You moving in?" I ask.

"Not today." From the top of the bag, she pulls out a tiny pair of blue striped pajamas. "Baby clothes. Mom got them from my cousin, Mari Carmen."

"All of them?"

"Yep. Her baby is such a *gordito*." She holds up a tiny undershirt. "He'd look like the Incredible Hulk if he squeezed into this now."

I pull out some tiny sweat pants from the other bag. "I love your mom."

Bree rolls her eyes. "You don't have her shaking Comet in your face all day long, telling you to clean something else."

I hold up a white sailor's outfit. "Is this for a girl or a boy?"

"I think it works for both," says Bree.

During the ultrasound the baby moved around so much the technician said she wasn't one hundred percent sure, but about seventy-five percent sure it's a girl. I pull out a pair of overalls. They look like a sunny day, like fishing at the river, like teasing Lyde for wearing dorky waders and him tossing grass into my hair.

"Have you talked to Lyde?" I ask.

She pulls out a blue T-shirt. "You know Lyde. It takes him a while to figure stuff out."

I set the overalls on top of the bag. "Well, he's hardly doing what his preacher is talking about all the time, *loving your enemies* and *doing good to the despicable*."

"You're hardly enemies. And I think the preacher said *despitefully use you,* not the despicable, that's a movie. And

191

just because someone goes to church, doesn't mean they don't mess up too."

"Well, he's always mowing some old lady's lawn or hauling canned tuna to the food bank. I mean, yes, I was dumb for sleeping with Marcus. Stupid even. But what does Lyde have to figure out? I'm the one who's blown up the size of Canada. All he has to do is be a friend. Is it really that difficult, to be there for your friend?"

My neck aches from balancing the ridiculous fruit hat on my head, and we still have one more day of advertising the pineapple smoothies. I press the blender button, lift my leg, and rotate my swollen ankle around. I've only been working an hour, but I'm already sore from head to toe.

"Do you see the line? We've got to move faster," complains Joe as he walks by.

"I'm blending as fast as possible," I say.

We're crazy busy all afternoon long trying to keep up with the Saturday crowd.

Finally, we get a break and no one's in line. Joe takes a clipboard back to the supply room, and I grab some cleaning spray and a towel and go over to the booths. Spray and wipe. I glance back. I'm so tired, I could fall asleep right here. I slide into the booth and heave my swollen feet up on the other side.

Cassandra walks over and starts cleaning off the table.

"Just give me a minute," I say.

"Stay. Take it easy," she says, staring at my stomach. My yellow uniform shirt is button-popping across the stomach. "Joe's lousy at scheduling breaks."

She flutters around, wiping down each of the tables.

"Hello?" calls out a guy waiting by the cash register. "Hello?"

I push myself up and try not to waddle as I move around the counter. "Welcome to Just Juice. Would you like to try a pineapple smoothie?" I say, trying to sound cheery, but it comes out sounding robotic.

"Hope I didn't interrupt your nap," he says, joking, but it's right as Joe comes out of the supply room.

"Ha! Good one," I say, but Joe still gives me a squinty look.

After another hour my legs are swelling. Joe pulls down the clattering metal cage, closing the store, but we still have to clean and restock. We finally finish and I'm about to lie down on the floor and go to sleep, when Cassandra asks, "You want to go grab a burger or a burrito or anything that's not fruity?"

"No, thanks, I'm beat."

Joe steps out of the supply room. "Melina, I need to see you in my office." I look over at Cassandra. With her back to Joe, she rolls her eyes, then pats my arm. "Don't you mind him; being manager has gone to his head," she whispers.

Joe's "office" is really the supply room with a couple of folding chairs that are usually stuck behind the door. He sits in one and I sit in the other. Like every day, he wears a shirt and tie, tucked neatly under a yellow apron. I cross my arms over, hiding my stomach and ask, "Why don't you wear the fruit hat?"

"They're for employees, not management."

"If they're to increase sales, shouldn't everyone wear them?"

With two fingers, he pats down his mustache. "We're not here to talk about the dress code. We're having some problems here at work."

"What problems?"

His eyes keep drifting down to my stomach. "I like to keep a certain atmosphere around here."

"Atmosphere?"

"Everything needs to be just so. Supplies in order. Counters gleaming."

"I work as hard as anyone to keep it that way."

"I can't have things out of place. You spill stuff, you're tired all the time, and well, you're bursting out of that uniform."

So that was it. Blah, blah, blah, on he goes. He tries to package the message up in a nice little gift box. I need "time to rest" and cutting my work hours down to almost nothing will be "beneficial for everyone." He doesn't come right out and say it but we both know what he meant: He runs a tight ship and the pregnant girl is being thrown overboard.

Church

After school I go out and start my car. Dad made some adjustments, checking tubes and connections and stuff and got it running. Joe didn't schedule me for work, so all I have is pages and pages of late homework to do. I keep driving, out past my old grade school, past 7-Eleven, past the cinderblock storage place.

I turn into the parking lot of Lyde's church and stop in the farthest parking spot from the door. I didn't mean to drive here, but here I am. Lyde's truck is parked by the front with a couple other cars. Maybe they're packing up more tuna or getting ready to go visit some old people. I wish I could go inside. But I can't. Not where the preacher talks about love and waiting and forever. All those people in there would look at me, at my stomach, and they'd know in an instant I wasn't listening at all.

I hear a squawk-honk and lean up to look out. A flock

of geese fly above me in the sky. They flap and glide and stick together like they know right where they're going.

Tap. Tap. There's a knock—the preacher—knocking on my window. I want to crank the engine, slam it into reverse, and peel out of there. But there he is with that smile, waving hello. I lower the window a few inches.

"Melina, so good to see you again."

"Oh, hi."

"Won't you come inside?"

"No, I'm sorry." I shake my head. "I can't."

"Please, just for a moment."

"I don't think so."

"How about we talk out here for a moment."

His eyes look so kind, and he speaks so soft: he's the hardest preacher to say no to. I get out and we sit there on that bench. I yank on my sweatshirt so it hides my stomach.

And the preacher shakes my hand.

And the preacher doesn't look at my seven-months-big stomach.

And the preacher says, we miss you and I wish you would come back.

And for just a minute I forget what a giant mess I'm in. For the tiniest moment, I think maybe it's okay for someone like me to be here.

Sunday

I close my eyes as I take a bite of Dad's homemade waffles slathered in butter and real maple syrup. Another delicious Sunday brunch. Belgian waffles and sausage links don't fix everything, but it's hard to stay one-hundred-percent mad when your mouth is full of deliciousness.

"What's on the agenda today?" he asks.

"Just homework."

"I'm showing houses this morning, but we could go to a movie later."

"I'm still really behind in school."

"Pizza, bowling, something else?"

"Bowling? I'd look ridiculous."

"Well, I'd like to do something together."

"Maybe."

When Dad takes off, I plop down on the couch, grab the remote, and start flipping through shows. The preacher invited me to Sunday service and for some weird reason, I said I'd think about it. The baby twirls and kicks inside me. What am I supposed to do, go to church and give all those people with their songbooks something to stare at?

I thump my foot against the coffee table and check the clock. Church will be starting soon. *Thump, Thump, Thump.* I hold onto my stomach. Am I too big and obvious? Or if I wear the right thing, will no one know?

I'm only a few minutes late when I sneak inside the church. While the congregation is singing, "What a Friend We Have in Jesus," I slip into the last row, right behind a big solid guy.

I hear a guitar and drums and peek around the big guy. There—up on stage— is Lyde! He's strumming that guitar, soft and smooth like he's out casting a fishing line. Next to him, his friend Jason is playing the keyboard, and a girl keeps beat with the drums. Also, up there is an older lady, waving her arms back and forth, directing the singing. I try to stay hidden behind the guy, but it doesn't seem to matter because Lyde's concentrating on the strumming.

We get to the end of the song, and the lady raises her arms slowing everyone down. *Oh what needless pain we bear, all because we do not carry.* She slows down even more… *everything to God in prayer.* She keeps her arms stretched out, making everyone hold that last note for an eternity.

Finally, she drops her arms, and Lyde gives a swooping last strum of the guitar. The lady shuts her songbook, and everyone in the band walks off the stage. For a brief moment it doesn't matter that Lyde and I haven't talked for months: I just want to run up and hug him and tell him it's so fabulous he plays in the church band, and then I want to shove him for not telling me about it before. I would've come sooner if I'd known he played in the band.

I shift, peering around. Lyde goes to sit with his family. His little brother is turned around, dancing a Batman figure across the back of the chair. What will Lyde do if he sees me? Grab his keys and hurry out the door or come shake my hand and give me a fake smile?

Today, the preacher wears a suit. He walks up and stands behind a wooden podium. I think he's looking at me when he says, "I'm grateful to see so many here today."

He flips pages in his Bible, and for a moment it's like he's looking past all of us. Like he isn't noticing an old woman folding a handkerchief over and over on her lap, a guy yawning, or a kid coloring on the back of the church bulletin.

The preacher begins. "You are a child of God. He knows your struggles. He feels your pain. He wants to heal you." He picks up his Bible, cradling it in his hands. "From the book of Matthew, Jesus says: 'Come unto me all ye that are heavy laden and I will give ye rest.'"

His voice is soft and gentle. "The Savior beckons us… come unto me, come here,

come home."

His words stack up, like words that can stand tall and shine through any storm—lighthouse words.

Rows ahead, Lyde's little brother sees me and starts waving. He waves so hard the Batman flies out of his hand. Some lady hands it back, and he starts poking Lyde in the shoulder.

I shake my head. No! I don't want Lyde to think I'm stalking him. I'm here because the preacher invited, that's all. The preacher said it would be okay. I try to duck behind the big guy.

But Lyde swivels around and looks at me, his eyes wide. In surprise? Shock? Horror?

I slip out of my seat, walk to the door, and rush outside.

The File

The weather's turned from cold to hot. The local news says it's an *uncanny heat wave, unheard of for this time of year.* But they should call it a *canny heat wave* because it's like I'm sweltering in a tin can. I keep pushing on the knob but the fan is broken and keeps swiveling. I sit and sweat and wait for the moments of breeze that come and go.

I'm supposed to write an essay for English but I can't concentrate. I go pick up a file of papers the preacher dropped by. *Just in case you're considering this option,* he said. The file has information about adoption websites, and there's also a stack of family profiles of people who want to adopt.

Dad comes out of the kitchen, wiping his hands on his apron. "You know Uncle Charlie is adopted."

"Yeah, I know."

"It's something to think about," says Dad, as he walks back into the kitchen.

I've heard the story over and over. My uncle, the one who complains anytime the temperature gets above 70. The one who dares me to jump waves with him out in the frigid Oregon coast. The one I'll live close to if I ever make it to Portland State University. Grandma called him her "miracle baby." After Dad, Grandma couldn't have any more kids; and she kept praying until she found Charlie to adopt. Charlie was a sickly, preemie baby who grew up to tower over my dad. Grandma always said, "Charlie dropped out of heaven."

What about Uncle Charlie's other mom, the one whose stomach swelled all up? What kind of mess was she in if she sent Charlie to be raised by someone else? No one ever mentions her. No one says a word about her. Did she think that Charlie dropped out of heaven?

I flip through the family profiles. I've read them all and looked at others online, a pile of prayers.

"May God bless you at this difficult time."

"We are a loving couple who desire to raise a child…"

"May the Lord guide and bless you."

"Whatever you decided, may God keep you."

It seems so wrong, so many people hoping for a baby. Then… how? In some flash of a moment this one landed with me. I flip the file closed and set it down.

It's impossible. Placing a baby for adoption would be like my mom packing her suitcase and leaving me. I won't do that. I won't have my baby wondering all the time, *what's wrong with me? Why did my mom leave me?*

The Day

Frank waits by my locker. My back aches and I didn't sleep much last night. I try to ignore him, but he's just there staring at me, there while I fumble with the dial. I mess up my combination twice. "What is it?" I say, after finally getting it right and yanking open the latch.

"It's about Marcus," he says, leaning in.

"What about him?" I haven't talked to Marcus in weeks, maybe even a month. Dad and I tried to meet with him and his mom. But at the last minute, his mom didn't show, and Marcus just sat there staring out the window, answering *I don't know* to every question.

"He's a mess."

All I want is to go collapse in a chair.

"He's got problems." Frank stares at my stomach. "And they're blowing up and getting out of control."

I grab my book and hold it with both hands, wishing I had enough guts to clobber Frank over the head with it.

"All Marcus does is work on the farm moving irrigation line and baling hay. He won't go out with us anymore."

"Marcus has problems?" I repeat.

Frank nods.

The ache in my back spreads out, like it's on an express train zooming through every nerve and right then, it pushes through a dam of things I've been holding in. "Let me guess. His stomach has grown so much that the only thing that fits are his dad's old polo shirts? And sometimes his legs swell so much they look like a hippopotamus's? And let's see what else, that every day he has to listen to his mom say, *you don't have the slightest idea of what you're getting into*?"

For a second, Frank keeps quiet and I think, maybe I did it, I got him to leave me alone. But then he shakes his head back and forth, like he's erasing every word I just said. He steps closer. "Marcus won't tell his recruiter. He's afraid he'll be rejected from the Air Force. You should talk to him, help him out."

My whole body shakes. "And what about me? Who's helping me? Who's going to the doctor's with me while they stick needles in my arms and take blood out." I try to slam my locker shut, but Frank holds it open.

"You should help him out."

Should. There are a lot of *shoulds.* One hundred *shoulds* all pile up on top of each other, like a giant tower. I *should've* gone straight home that night, or we *should've* used a condom. Most of all, I *shouldn't* have fallen for him in the first place. "Who is helping me?"

"You'll ruin his life!" he shouts. And with that, everyone in the school seems to stop. And a whole giant crowd freezes in the hall, watching us like we are the Friday night game.

"Go away, Frank."

"Come on, Melina."

There's a blur and someone shoves in. Suddenly, there is Lyde, right between us. "Hey, what's going on?"

"We're talking," says Frank.

"I'm done talking," I say, and try to shut my locker again. Frank holds it fast. "Not yet."

Lyde stays right there and stands up, right in Frank's face. "Back off," Lyde growls.

Frank doesn't budge.

"Leave Melina alone," says Lyde.

"We're having a conversation, so why don't you take off?" says Frank.

"I'm not leaving," says Lyde.

And now the crowd starts percolating. "Fight," says someone.

"Hit him," says another.

And then more and more voices break in. "Fight, fight, fight." A crazy chant starts, like this is some kind of en-

207

tertainment. Lyde stands there with this look in his eyes and Frank glares back. They look like a couple of mountain goats ready to buck each other's horns off. Lyde steps closer. Frank clenches his hands into fists. This is for real. The school has a zero-tolerance policy. Fighting can mean suspension or even expulsion from school, and I won't let Lyde do that for me.

"Hey! Stop! I'm pregnant!" I yell. Wait. What did I just say? Lyde and Frank both look back and forth, as confused as I am. But shoot, I decide to roll with it. "Yeah, that's right. I'm pregnant."

Someone in the crowd gasps, which is so stupid. Everyone's known about me for months. I'm old news by now. "Okay," I announce loud enough for everyone to hear. "I know you're fighting over who gets to babysit first, but there's no need. You'll both get plenty of turns to babysit."

Frank blinks.

Lyde stares. I grab him by the arm and yank but he stands his ground.

Announcing the pregnancy out loud, in some way, makes me feel strong. Somehow, now I feel like an open book. Fine. I have nothing to hide. Forget Bree—I'm in the spotlight now. "Come on, Lyde. I've got to go to class, graduate, get a job, and support this baby. No one else is going to do it."

Lyde looks at me like I'm crazy and maybe I am. But

there will be no fight today, no suspension or expulsion. None of that is happening on my watch. I start pulling him down the hallway, and he lets me.

"What was that?" He shakes his head, like he's coming out of hypnosis.

"I'm not sure," I say, which is one-hundred-percent true.

"Was that some kind of performance?" The corners of his mouth twitch, a smile is bubbling up.

"I guess it was all those hours practicing with Bree," I say, grinning too.

"Bree better watch out. With performances like that you'll take the part of Dorothy, for sure," says Lyde.

"Auntie Em… Auntie Em… Toto," I say, and we crack up, all the way down the hall.

Biology Class

All morning long my back hurts. Probably because all last night I tossed around in bed. I dreamed I was a mermaid stuck in a subway, flopping around and not able to get to the ocean. And the night before I dreamed a giant chicken was chasing me through the city, Godzilla-like.

I shift in my seat in biology class, wishing for a heating pad, when a student runner comes in and hands Mr. Denslow a yellow paper.

"Melina," he says, hardly glancing up from taking attendance. I twist out of my seat, trying not to waddle like a pregnant girl with a hurting back, and take the notice from his hand. This time the note from Mr. Garret, the school counselor, says: *Come in immediately.*

I guess this is what you get after ignoring four other notes. What will he do next? Show up, snap handcuffs on my wrists, and haul me away? I fold the paper into a rectangle and stick it deep into my back pocket.

Mr. Denslow stands up. "Okay, it's the day you've all been waiting for. Move quietly to the lab tables, and follow the procedures exactly as outlined on the whiteboard."

Everyone shuffles to the back without much noise. Denslow is no softie. He hung his old fraternity paddle above the whiteboard, and always talks about the *good old days*, wishing he was a teacher back when you could paddle students instead of send them to detention.

Bree follows and I rub my back muscles as I walk.

"What's going on?" she whispers.

"It's just a backache and some cramps."

She grabs my arm. "Maybe this is it. What if you're going into labor?"

I shrug her away. "It's impossible."

"Melina. I've been studying births on YouTube. It can happen anywhere—at restaurants, on buses, even at schools."

"I'm not even close yet." I sit down at the lab table on one of the stools.

Bree sits, takes out her purple pen, and folds back the notebook. "I'll do the note-taking."

"You're not scared of a worm are you?" I ask.

"It's disgusting."

I stretch on a pair of gloves and pull the worm out of a bag.

"*Cómo huele*," she says, holding her nose and fanning the air in front of her.

211

She's right. The smell of formaldehyde is horrible. I take the probe and start counting the rings.

"I can't watch."

"Oh, come on." Pain shoots through my back and all of a sudden my underwear feels wet. I drop the probe and it clangs on the counter. "Something's wrong."

Bree peeks through her fingers. "The thing's already dead. How could something be wrong?"

"No, with me. Something's wrong with me."

Bree puts down the notebook. "Heartburn?"

"No."

"Do you need to throw up?"

"Listen, I've gotta go." I slide off my stool and hurry to the door.

"Wait."

I grab the hall pass hanging by the door and Mr. Denslow merely nods. One benefit of being pregnant, the teachers will let you use the pass anytime.

As I hurry down the hall, I hear Bree talking behind me. "She's feeling sick. And in her condition, I don't think she should be left alone."

More pain pummels my back. Is this some weird symptom at seven months? What did Dr. Kate say was normal? Gas and bloating—this is more than that. She never said anything about back-slamming pain.

I make it to the bathroom, bang the stall door shut and

212

slide the latch closed. I yank down my sweats. Bright red blood covers my underwear. Blood. Blood isn't good, is it? I'm not supposed to bleed.

"Melina?" Bree's voice rings through the bathroom. "You okay?"

"I'm bleeding."

"Bleeding?"

"Bleeding like a period." I wrap toilet paper around and around my shaking hand and stuff the wad in my underwear. I open the door, start to wash my hands, but when a stinging pain shoots through my back, I have to grab onto the sink sides.

"Do you think it's serious?"

"How am I supposed to know?"

"We have to call your doctor."

I know she's right so I grab my phone out of my pocket and call the doctor's office. Doctor Kate isn't in, but the nurse's voice is crisp and clear. "Get to the hospital immediately."

Nada

At first, I'm stuck alone in the hospital room. Out the window, the clouds sit there unmoving and the sky looks a pale, sickly blue. Dad left to go fill out papers, and a temporary nurse came in, stuck me with a needle to get blood, and then took off, saying my regular nurse would be there in a minute.

Next to the window, some curtains hang down. They've got rubber ducks on them, but the ducks look startled, like they just realized they're headed for a waterfall.

"I'm Daisy," says the new nurse, when she comes in. She smells like vanilla and there's a pen stuck in her brown hair. "Let's check your blood pressure." She takes the stethoscope off a hook and puts it in her ears.

I flex my arm.

"Try to relax."

"Now," she says slowly and calmly. "I've called your doctor."

"When will Dr. Kate get here?" I ask. Everything will be better once she's here.

"Your blood pressure is elevated. We need to keep an eye on that." Daisy pivots the computer screen over and puts in my score. "Sorry, hon. Your doctor is out of town."

"But she'll be back, won't she? Later today."

She shakes her head. "Not for a few days, I'm afraid. But the doctor on call, Doctor Michelson, he's a very good doctor."

I sit up. "He? I don't want a man doctor. That's why I chose Dr. Kate. She's supposed to be here."

Nurse Daisy puts a warm hand on my arm. "Don't you worry at all. I'll be right here. Everything's going to be fine."

I sink back into the pillow. On the countertop, there is a jar of throat sticks for gagging patients. Next to that, a red plastic cylinder with the word "BIOHAZARD" in giant letters. Dr. Kate was supposed to help me. And now I'm stuck with a man. Checking me down there.

This isn't right. Why is this happening to me? Marcus was there too. I mean we did this together. He should be here. He should be made to change out of his clothes and wear a flimsy hospital gown. He should be the one lying here, getting stuck with needles and staring out the window. The one who's grown as big as Mexico, and, now, who's stuck with some man doctor.

What happened to Marcus?

Nada. Absolutely *nada.*

Pain

Before, it felt like cramps. Easy, take-an-Ibuprofen cramps. But now, it's a wave. A wave of people. A huge stadium full of people. At first, they jab my back with their fists. Millions pound into me. Then they use their feet. A million feet stomp wearing steel-toed boots. And suddenly it's sledgehammers. Thick, iron sledgehammers. They pound my back. Faster and faster. I close my eyes, squeezing them until everything is blackness.

I try to think about something else. I imagine running the path alongside the river, but the sledgehammers don't stop. They don't care about me or the river. My arms squeeze to my sides. Every muscle feels rigid and tight. Get me away. Make them stop.

I feel a squeeze at my shoulder. "*Ándale* girl, you've got this," says Bree.

"No! I don't." I shake my head. The stadium people put down the sledgehammers. But they go back to kicking.

Stomping with their boots. A demented dance. Then back to fists. Punching. Then they put their arms down. It's over. I open my eyes.

"Ice?" asks Bree, holding a plastic spoon and ice nugget to my lips.

I push it away. "No."

Before labor started, Daisy asked who I wanted in here. I told her just Bree—she'd been getting ready for this, watching Grey's Anatomy and asking all of her aunts for advice.

The pain starts again. My body tenses and I squeeze my eyes shut. The stadium full of people thunder back. Oh please, please, no. Just let me die. This time, they have swords. Giant steel swords that have been set on fire. They plunge the sticks into my back and stomach.

"Breathe," says Daisy. "Let your body do the work."

"You're doing *fabulosa*. You're a rockstar," says Bree.

I breathe in something strong and flowery.

"*Respira,* Mel. Relax. In through your nose, out through your mouth." I open my eyes to see Bree spraying a tiny bottle. "My *Tia* said lavender will release nervous tension."

"This is *not* nervous tension!" I want to throw the big hospital phone at Bree's head. The people with their boots and sledgehammers are coming back. They aren't here yet, but I know they're coming. Daisy checks the monitor behind me. I want out of this sick game. Is there a coach

218

somewhere? Anywhere? Please, someone, tell the coach to take me out. Please send in a sub.

A man comes in wearing scrubs with an American flag bandana over his head, making him look half-doctor and half-biker. "Someone in here want an epidural?"

"Yes," I say, not even caring that he sounds so lame.

"Can you roll over on your side?" he asks.

"Sure," I say, my voice cracking. I'll do whatever. I'll stand on my head and sing, "*My Country 'Tis of Thee*" if he'll get the pain to go away.

Daisy helps me roll over.

"Hold on now, just give me a few moments and you'll feel much better," says Bandana Doctor. Behind me, I hear a rattling, that tray on wheels.

Bree's at my feet. "Listen, Mel, I... It's my watch. I forgot my watch. Maybe it's in the car." She moves towards the door. "I've got to have it. So I can time the contractions." The hospital door thuds behind her before I can ask her what's wrong with the clock on her phone.

Hurry, hurry. The people with their boots are coming.

"Go to your happy place," says Daisy. On the wall is a poster about breastfeeding. A baby clamps down on a giant, fat breast like it is a hamburger. My happy place is *El Mercado*, with Mexican pastries, going there with my two best friends.

As the sweet, cold medicine sinks into me, I hear the

door open again. Stuck on my side, I can't turn to look. Bree? The tap of heels on the floor. Quickly, I take in the high heels, straight skirt, jacket, a pained smile. "Mom?" She smooths back my hair. "You're here?"

"Of course." She kisses me right on the top of my head. And even though the people are returning, slamming their sledgehammers into me, I smile back at her and close my eyes to fight.

"It will take a few minutes for the medicine to go into full effect," says Bandana Doctor.

Mom squeezes my arm. "This baby is coming earlier than we thought."

"That's how some babies are. They have a mind of their own," says Daisy.

"They certainly do," says Mom.

Arrival

I clutch Mom's hand.

Take in a deep breath.

Hold in my air.

Daisy says, "Okay, hon, you really are finally there. Push."

I squeeze my eyes tight until there's total blackness.

Daisy counts, "1…"

I push.

"2…"

And push.

"3…"

And push some more.

"4…"

Until there is nothing inside. I am done. Empty. I exhale. My head flops onto the pillow.

Bree puts a hand on my shoulder. "Girl, you've got this." Her words come out in a raspy whisper. Ten hours ago, she had a voice. Now she sounds like she should be admitted to the hospital herself.

"Sweetie. Let's go again," says Daisy.

"Melina, you can do this," says Mom.

My body wants to push.

Forget it.

Leave me alone.

It's been too long.

I'm done.

I can't do this anymore.

"I can't."

"You can," says Daisy.

The man, who is not Doctor Kate, peeks out from the spotlighted area. "She's crowning."

I look up at Daisy. Sweat drops race down the side of her face.

"Crowning?"

"It means he can see the top of the head. You are so close. Okay hon, take a couple of quick breaths and give us one more push."

I do it for Daisy.

"Great job, hon, you're an expert." She wipes my forehead with a cloth.

There is pressure. All kinds of pressure down there.

I clamp my teeth together. My back is wet with sweat. Get me out of here. I don't want to be here. With one hand

I squeeze Mom's hand and the other I press hard into the mattress.

"Head is out," says the doctor.

"One more push."

I push until there is nothing left.

"Here she is," says the doctor and lifts up the baby for less than a second, then holds her back down again.

I see a flash, a glimpse of purple skin.

I sink deep into the bed.

I can't see her.

I see scissors. The doctor cuts the cord.

Where is the cry?

"I hate it when they hold their breath," he says.

I bend forward, trying to see.

Babies are supposed to cry, right?

Mom's hand in mine goes limp.

I look at Bree. Her face is a pile of sand, blowing away.

I grab Bree's arm, squeezing and pressing. "What's going on?" She turns and stares out the window.

"I don't…" I let go of Bree's arm. Why isn't the baby crying?

Daisy hits a button.

The doctor is doing stuff.

Scooping out her mouth. Rubbing her back.

The door slams open. Four people burst in.

But there should be noise shouldn't there? In all the TV shows, the baby cries.

The doctor places the baby on the small table and the four people move in and surround her. They all have their heads down.

I still can't see. Daisy comes over and gives my head a one-arm hug. She moves, checking the monitor.

"Is she okay?" I ask.

No one answers.

Daisy squeezes my arm.

Mom stands frozen, her hand on the bed rail.

I turn away from the whispering people. The room is cold. My sweatshirt lies listless on the rocking chair. Blinds on the window hang, unmoving.

Silence.

I don't even shift. My heart slams around in my chest. Wanting to break out. Wanting to run away.

Daisy presses buttons on the monitor.

The door opens and Dad peeks in, his face white.

Mom shakes her head and he backs out.

I stare at the clock. There is no second hand. What happened to the second hand? It used to have a second hand. It should be moving. It blurred away.

I crane my neck trying to see. But all of those blue scrubs are in the way. A wall shielding me from seeing.

Why doesn't Bree move from the window?

What is happening?

Daisy presses on my stomach. She whispers, "One more tiny push."

"Okay," I say, in the smallest whisper.

The doctor is doing something down there. I don't know. It doesn't matter. What matters is the silence that fills up the room.

Rushing

And then a cry.

A big, loud, screaming cry. Like the sound of a rushing river.

I gasp for air.

She's crying!

Mom finally brings her hand down from her mouth. She puts it on my head and holds it there.

Bree leaves the window and hurries over to hold my hand. The doctor walks over. His mouth moves and he's saying a bunch of words. A big bunch of words with his big, fat mouth. I don't know what he is saying because all I can hear is that beautiful cry.

A nurse brings the baby over, wrapped in a blanket. I stroke her dark, matted hair. And stare at that little red mouth that is open and crying. Before I have a chance to hold her, while I'm still reaching out, the nurse with the baby turns away.

"Wait," I say.

The nurse puts the baby in the bassinet with wheels and with two other people, one on each side, they wheel her off.

"I'm sorry, we must get the baby to the NICU as soon as possible," says one of them.

Dad comes in. "Did you see her?" I ask.

"I sure did. She's beautiful."

Mom holds on to the bedrail. "Wow. Wow. Wow."

"*Increíble*," says Bree.

Mom, Bree, Dad and I, we all look at the door.

I try to push myself up. "Will someone follow them? Someone has to go and make sure that she's okay." Bree and Dad hurry out.

Mom is still here next to me. In this whole time, she hasn't moved, not to go get a drink or go to the bathroom. She's been right here through everything. She smooths my hair and sticks a loose strand behind my ear. "Melina, you are amazing. You handled everything so well."

Nurse Daisy wraps my arm with the black band to take my blood pressure.

I look up at Mom. "How did you get here?"

She smiles. "First by plane, then an Uber."

"You came, just like that?"

"The second your dad called, I grabbed my purse, ran out of the office, and sped all the way to the airport."

"You didn't go to your apartment?"

"There wasn't time."

"Or pack a bag?"

She shook her head. "None of that mattered. Just making it here in time to be with you. That's what I had to do."

I lean back and close my eyes, feeling the warm sun that pours in through the window. Mom came, without any of her work files, without a change of clothes or even a toothbrush. She came to be with me.

Baby

I grip the side of the crib and look down. The baby has tubes in her nose and one in her hand. There are wires attached to her tiny chest and one to her foot. Every part of her is hooked to machines. I watch her tiny stomach, making sure it keeps moving up and down, up and down.

Oh, please, God. What did I do? The man doctor said the baby had to be delivered. That we couldn't wait and that she must come right away. Is this my fault? Did I make her come early? I didn't always take those giant vitamins that made me gag. And I didn't cut down on the hours I was working. I kept going even when my feet swelled up. And then… please God, I'm so sorry. There were the times I didn't want her. Times I wished I wasn't pregnant. Days that I dreamed the baby would disappear. But now here she is.

Gorgeous, oh she is gorgeous. Black hair pokes out

around her head like exclamation points. Please God, make her be okay.

The nurse with her glasses on a dangling chain comes over carrying another IV bag. She releases the flattened bag and hooks up the new one.

"Her heart is beating really fast," I say.

The nurse nods.

"And the tube in her nose."

"It's fine."

"And there's so much beeping going on."

The nurse places her hand on my shoulder and squeezes. But it's only for a moment, and then she walks away.

I go back to my room and sleep a few hours. When the sun starts to blink in my window, I grab my bathrobe and shuffle my sore body over to the NICU. Mom is here. Last night she slept in my room on a chair that folds out. She wears the same black skirt and pinstriped blouse as yesterday. Dad came first thing too. They both look up from the bassinet when I hurry in.

"The doctor was just here doing rounds," says Mom.

"What did he say?" I ask. The baby is sleeping with her little hand pressed up against her cheek.

"They're still monitoring her breathing," she says.

I sit down. For hours I sit there, not even rocking so I can keep my eyes on her. Dad wanders in and out. Mom stays most of the morning and then has to go call her office.

The nurse comes over and checks the monitor. "Have you held her yet?"

I shake my head.

She looks again at the monitor. "It's approved. You should hold her."

"What if I hurt her?"

She gives me a soft smile. "As long as you're careful with the oxygen and IV placement, it will be all right."

My heart pounds as I sit there and the nurse slowly lifts the baby out of the bassinet and places her in my arms, looping the oxygen tube around my shoulder.

"Oh." The sound slips out as I hold her close, as gentle as a whisper. One hand peeks out from the blanket and I stroke her skin with my finger. She stares at me and I barely rock her, careful for the tubes.

May, that's what I will call her. May. Her name came to me like a penny sliding into its spot in a coin sorter.

Amigos

When the nurse returns, she says, "Why don't we put her back in her bassinet?"

"Already?"

"It's been half an hour," she says softly.

I can't believe it's been so long. In the hospital time seems to move at a warped speed, slowing down or speeding up, going whichever way you don't want it to. The nurse holds the tubes as I lift May into the bassinet.

A little later, Mom comes in. She smiles at May as she holds onto the edge of the bassinet. "Bree and Lyde are here to see you."

"Where? They have to see her."

"They don't have clearance for the NICU; it's just me and your dad."

"Oh, sure," I say, feeling like I should've remembered that.

"You should go and visit with them."

"But who's going to watch the baby?"

"I'll stay here with the baby. They've been waiting for hours."

"Really?"

"They arrived first thing this morning."

"Okay," I say, walking away. "I won't be gone too long." In the waiting room, all the chairs are empty, except for two. Bree and Lyde have their backs to me. She has her head on his shoulder, while he flips through pages in a magazine. And for some reason, seeing them both sitting so close, suddenly I remember how much hospitals make me queasy. "Geez, can't I go anywhere to get away from you two?"

They turn around, pop out of their chairs, and give me giant hugs. Bree holds my arms and steps back, like she's examining me. "*Pobrecita*, how are you?" I guess in a hospital gown and bathrobe, I do look like a poor thing.

I shrug. *How am I?* I'm every emotion and I'm not sure which one will come up next.

"You look good," says Lyde.

"You've always been a rotten liar," I say, smiling.

"I'm serious," he says.

"Where's the baby?" asks Bree. "Can we see her?"

"No, she's sick. She has to stay in the NICU."

"Here, you should sit down." Lyde pulls three chairs

233

around in a circle. We sit down and he hands me a purple box wrapped with a big white ribbon.

"Nice wrapping."

Lyde points to Bree. "Purple and white, go Bulldogs," she says. "Now, open it."

I tear off the paper, open the box and pull out a small baby t-shirt with pink lettering. It says: *The Fourth Amigo.*

"Ha!" I laugh and hold it up.

"We've planned it out," says Bree. "I will teach her how to act, sing, and dance." She thumbs over at Lyde. "And he can teach her how to fish."

I put the shirt back in the box. "Who knows? Maybe she'll like pole vaulting or scuba diving."

"I'm sure she'll like fishing," says Lyde, grinning wide. "I'll teach her the right way to cast."

At first, I smile so big, picturing a little girl in fishing waders walking around with Lyde and then dancing with Bree. But then, something feels off. I stare at that baby T-shirt and everything blurs in confusion. I sit and stare and stare, not knowing what to do.

Bree leans of and reaches for my hands. "Hey, Mel. It's going to be okay." She holds my hands and rubs them softly.

"Yeah, Mel, the three amigos, one for all and all that crap," says Lyde, winking and grabbing one of my hands too.

Can we do really do it? Will the three of us make a family for May? I flash them a fast smile and then slowly stand up, feeling as heavy as a hippo. "I better get back. You guys are the best." I hold tight to that gift and shuffle back down the hall.

Dad

When I return to the NICU, the nurse's eyes shine as she says they've taken out the IV. May still needs oxygen, but she's doing better. As I look down at her hand, now free from one of the tubes, I want to run around and bang on everyone's hospital door and tell them the good news. I lean over and whisper, "You can do this, May. You're a fighter."

Later, the nurse helps me to feed May. She hands me the tiny bottle and helps hold the oxygen cord out of the way. Her pink mouth opens and she chomps onto that bottle like a pro.

"Prop her head up," says the nurse.

I shift, holding her up. "Like this?"

"You're doing great."

While May sucks and sucks on that bottle, Dad comes in and sits down.

"I'm proud of you. You're doing an amazing job," he says.

"They took out the IV. She's doing better."

"She looks wonderful."

"I'm naming her May,"

"Beautiful. I like it."

I nod.

"I wish they had a piano here, so I could play her a lullaby." He leans back in the chair and hums "All the Pretty Little Horses."

"Dad…"

"Yes."

"So, what happened with you and Mom?"

He takes his glasses off and rubs his hand over his face.

I wait, listening to the beep of the machines.

"Well, there's the obvious. I made the worst mistake of my life. But before that, it was all the smaller mistakes, not spending time together, having different goals, not realizing how important the job in Seattle was to her."

I rock May, back and forth.

"Selfishness, stupidity on my part."

I run my finger over May's silky hair. "What's going to happen between you two?"

He shrugs. "I don't know if she'll ever forgive me."

"But things used to be so good for all of us."

Dad nods and then he slides his chair over next to me. Careful for May's tube, he puts his arm around me. "They were honey. They really were."

"Can they ever be good again?"

"Maybe." He looks towards the door. "But I don't know. I'm sorry."

Me holding May, Dad holding me. I still don't get it. I don't understand how he could choose someone over me and Mom, even for a minute. But right then with his arm tight around me, I love him, even if I don't understand.

Visiting Hours

After a while Dad insists I go to my room to eat the dinner the nurse ordered for me. Turkey, mashed potatoes, corn and peas; I eat every single thing and still feel hungry. I shut the blinds and lie down on the bed.

The giant phone in my room rings. "Marcus Townsend is here. Would you like me to send him in?" asks a nurse.

"Marcus? Really?"

"Yes."

"Okay, send him in."

In a moment, the door cracks open and he peeks in. "Are you alone?"

"Yes." I press the button, so the bed moves to a sitting position.

He wanders around, touching the sink faucet, looking at the computer monitor, grabbing some latex gloves out of a box. Then he walks over and sits in the rocking chair.

"What are you doing here?" I ask, rubbing my neck, which suddenly feels so tight.

"I've never been in a hospital before."

"You wanted to see a hospital room?"

"I heard the baby is a girl."

I sit up. "She's sick, kind of. You can't go see her yet." What if he bumps her oxygen tube or something? "She's in the NICU."

He stares at the gloves in his hands. "Who does she look like?"

I could lie and tell him she's one-hundred-percent me, but she's not. She's part Marcus too. "She has your dark hair."

He nods. He stretches out the fingers on one of the gloves and starts blowing. When the glove looks like one giant fat hand, he ties the end. "Babies like balloons, right?"

I don't know what to say.

He blows up another one. "Now there's a pair." Marcus thumps the two balloon things together and then gazes out the window. "I should probably go."

"Aren't you coming back?"

He shrugs. "I start basic in a couple of weeks."

"We need to figure out stuff about the baby."

He stands up. "The recruiter said they'd take the child support out of my paycheck. So you can have that." He puts the balloons on the chair. "Here, you can give her those from me."

"Babies need more than money. Babies need their dads, too." They need dads that will swing them high up into the air and run around playing tickle monster. "When will you be back from basic?"

He looks down, like he's examining the wheels on the hospital bed. "Will you tell her? Tell the baby I came to see her, will you?"

Later that night, I stand next to the bassinet. I twist my finger into May's palm so that her curled fingers wrap around my finger, forcing her to cling to me. Is that what I wanted from Mom and Marcus, for them to cling to me?

I untwist my finger from May's hand because a baby shouldn't have to do that, should they? They should just get to crawl around and eat mashed-up stuff from a jar and have that happy grin on their face. They shouldn't have to make sure their mom is okay, should they? And deep inside I have this feeling of what I should do but it is too hard. It is too, too, hard. Please God, no one should ever have to do that too-hard thing.

I put my forehead down on the side of the bassinet and the drips coming down my face make little drops at my feet. And I pray to God to make this stop. To help me because there's no way that I can do this.

And I breathe hard, sucking in air and it's filling me up

and the tears kept slipping off my face and I don't know what to do.

Courtyard of Hope

Back in the NICU, I sit in a chair and watch as May's stomach goes up and down as she breathes. I want everything for her. One on each side to hold her hands and swing her high into the sky. And there it is again, that thing I won't think about. My heart thumps away almost as fast as May's. The bassinet and May go all blurry. But it can't be right if it makes me cry, can it?

The nurse comes over and looks at the monitor. "She's improving. You should go take a break."

My breasts and back and legs ache. I feel like I've been stomped on by an elephant and then forced to run a marathon, but I don't want to leave her side.

"You can't take care of your baby if you don't first take care of yourself. You need to rest."

The nurse waits as I push myself out of the chair. I step over to May, smooth out a crease in her hospital beanie and whisper, "I'll be right back."

My head feels light as I walk down the hallway. Lining the hall are posters of babies: one sucking on her fist, one staring out with big green eyes, one boy wearing a sail- or hat, but no pictures of sick babies. None with wires or tubes sticking in them.

I keep going. I turn down one hall and then another; each hallway is the same.

Am I the same?

Twenty hours ago, she was born. I stop and try to look at my reflection in the silver part of a fire extinguisher. Same hair, teeth, nose. But somewhere deep inside—no way am I the same.

Up ahead, at the end of the hallway, it looks like there's a forest. It's a green canopy of leaves and ivy painted above two double doors. On a wooden stand a sign says, *Court- yard of Hope.*

I push on the door and, before my eyes adjust, I take a step into the dark. Then I realize, I'm outside on a terrace. Lights hang from trees. A breeze fills the air with the smell of green things growing. Vines climb up a brick wall in the back. Ferns and lilies pour over flowerbeds. I walk farther in. Yellow roses climb up trellises. It's like a garden of Eden out here. Why didn't I see this place before? Why didn't anyone tell me about it?

I find my way over to a wicker chair and ease my sore body down. For a while I just sit, but then this seems like the perfect place for it, so I close my eyes and pray. *Dear God, please help me. I'm in a giant mess. How can I take care of May? And how could I possibly not take care of May and pass that on to someone else? God, are you there? Do you even care? Or listen? I've prayed before but I still don't even really know; are you even there?*

I wait and… there's nothing. No light shines down from above. No voice speaks from heaven. No angel appears. It's just me waiting.

Still Small

Later that night, I remember something the preacher said once. He quoted from the Bible about God *not* being in the wind, and God *not* being in the earthquake, and God *not* being in the fire. But that God *was* in a still, small voice.

I think about the people's voices that help me. The preacher, how he says, *God knows you and loves you.* And I think about Lyde who tells me, *you've got this, Mel.* And Mom who says, *you are amazing.* Maybe God softly speaks to us through other people.

And I remember the preacher saying we help God by helping others. And I think about Bree being by my side all through the birth and Mom who jumped on a plane without packing and Lyde who almost got in a fight. And I think about myself too, how I decided to have this baby when it was so hard. And wasn't God in all of that? If we are children of God, then isn't some of his DNA in us? Isn't he a part inside us that's cheering us on and helping us to do good?

And right now, there's no wind or earthquake or fire and there's not even any kind of voice in my head, but I feel my heart swelling and swelling and I know what I need to do for May.

Forever

No oxygen, no IV, the second morning in the hospital the doctors say May is ready to come out of the NICU. She is fine without any tubes or wires. I hold May alone in my room and rock her and wish that the world would stop spinning and that we could be just like this. Me holding her and pressing my lips against her soft hair, forever.

A Visit

The nurses keep coming in and checking her—oxygen levels, blood pressure, heart rate, they check everything. If anything changes, she'll have to go back to the NICU. Each time they check I'm so nervous, my hands sweat and I have to wipe them on my gown. But for now, May's staying with me. After a break for lunch, Mom and Dad come and sit in the room with me, taking turns holding May.

"Look at those legs," says Mom and she changes a diaper and May's legs kick and kick. Mom places May in the middle of a blanket, tucks in one corner and then the next and wraps her in a little cocoon. She sits in the rocker and gently rocks May. "She's beautiful."

"Isn't she?" I say.

"We're really proud of you," says Dad, and something warm fills me up.

"You've handled everything like a champ," says Mom. "You're much stronger than I thought you could ever be."

The thing in my chest keeps filling up.

"You'll be a great mom," she says, and then stares down at the floor.

And that warm swelling is even bigger.

"Thanks," I say. The words are there waiting. And what I need to say, to do, is growing inside of me. The words come out, painful words. "But I want something more for May."

Mom stops rocking.

Dad stops looking at his phone.

I have to look up. I can't do this alone. I stare up at the ceiling, and pray that God will help me. "More than I can give her."

There's one family in the preacher's file that stuck out. More than stuck out. I haven't been able to get their photo out of my mind.

Dad takes his glasses off, rubs his hand over his face, and then returns the glasses. He walks around the room, stuffing my duffle bag into an empty wardrobe closet, lining up the flower vases. He takes my empty dinner tray out of the room. Mom left with the excuse of making phone calls and checking in at the office. But the way she's taken to May, I think she's afraid to meet them.

I push out of the hospital bed and ease over to the tiny

hospital bassinet, feeling shaky and weak. I slide my thumb across her cheek. Of course, she's sleeping. I smile. She'll wait until later to be awake, until it's just us and I can hold her for hours.

I go to the window and rotate the blinds open. Below, a nurse walks away from the hospital. I hold onto the windowsill. Maybe it's her lunch break. I wish I were her, just an ordinary day, going out to lunch.

I go back to the bassinet and stare down at May. There's a knock on the door.

"Come in," I say.

The dad holds open the wide hospital door and she enters wearing a warm, wobbly smile. He ducks as he comes through the doorway, his hands clutching the sides of a cowboy hat.

She gives me a quick hug and I shake his hand. I looked at so many families. Photos, stories, and bios that had all sounded like prayers. But the words on their bio flowed into me like a river. A photo of the mom, dad, and a young boy standing in front of a weathered fence. A little brother, grinning like he'd just caught a ladybug.

Baby May would have an instant family.

"Would you like to see her?" I ask.

We all move to the bassinet. The couple stands side by side. Their hands wrap together.

May sleeps softly. They say she's *precious* and *beautiful*.

My dad and I agree. After a long time of staring, we all sit down. I'm in the rocking chair. They ask about my health and the delivery. My chair is warm, comfortable, and I rock softly. The cowboy wears new Wranglers and old boots. She's in jeans and a button-down shirt covered with the tiniest flowers. She smells like gingersnaps.

May squirms in her bassinet. "Would you like to hold her?" I ask. As I pick up May, she stretches one arm out, then snuggles into me.

"Absolutely," he says.

I hold May close to my heart. I press her there, whisper *I love you*, then pass her into his careful hands.

The sun peeks in through the window. All of baby May fits inside his giant cowboy hands. As he cradles her into his chest and holds her there, the room fills with light. He drags the sleeve of his western shirt under his eye as he holds onto May. The lady wraps her hands onto his arm. Their eyes don't drift off of baby May.

Decide

I don't think it's here at the hospital where I decide. I think somehow I knew it all along. Like knowing the plastic pee stick would show two lines. Like knowing that I couldn't stop her from coming. Like knowing the family is perfect for her. Like knowing, for me, her name will always be May.

When I tried to picture me and Marcus and May all I could see were those wings on his chest. I could try to make him. Force him into our lives. But as soon as he could, he'd be gone, leaving a white streak in the sky.

May deserves more than a disappearing white streak.

I know they're waiting. Watching the phone. Not letting anyone call. Maybe they're sorting socks or sweeping the floor, trying to keep their minds off of her.

Cradled in a cotton blanket, May's black hair pokes up around her head. I rub my lips against her silky hair and kiss the top. Then I pick up my phone.

She answers on the first ring.

The words come out smooth as a river rock. "I'm sure."

She'll be with them. I can start May off with two.

I only waited because no one wants to break her own heart on purpose.

Going Home

After we get home from the hospital, I walk straight back
to my bedroom, holding the teddy bear in my arms. At the
hospital, they gave me a weighted bear. One stuffed with
pebbles or sand or something so it's heavier, like a baby. Id-
iots. Like you can replace a baby with a bear. Still, though,
I hold onto it. I slide open my closet door. And in there, I
ease myself down. I slide the door shut and stay there in the
dark. Not wanting to talk to Dad or Mom. Not wanting to
see anyone. I curl up and gently press that bear to my chest.
Right in the middle. Right where I am breaking in two.

SUMMER

Phone Calls

The wind blows and blows. Sand particles fill the air and everything turns hazy. In the morning when Dad leaves for work, I stay in bed and sleep for hours, curling up into the smallest me possible.

Dad begs me every day, until after two weeks, I start going to work with him. The real-estate agents ask for help with soft eyes and low voices. I hold onto the copy machine, stare at the numbers on the screen and listen as it cranks and whirls.

I go to church. The ladies come up and wrap their arms around me and Lyde stays at my side. Sunday nights, I wait and say the same prayer over and over: *Please God, let May be okay*. And then, right as planned, right at seven p.m., the mom calls me. I always ask the same thing right off. "How is she? Is everything okay?"

And when she says, "May is perfect, absolutely perfect," I close my eyes and thank God.

September

The day I circled on the family calendar is finally here. The wind has stopped howling, and the sun pours in through my window. I kneel in front of my dresser, jiggle open the bottom drawer, and pull out the top envelope from a stack held together by a rubber band.

I hold tight to the letter, go outside and jog, light and loose to the end of our street. I keep going, flying past all the houses, pressing into each step. Moving up one street and then another. The sun warms my shoulders and a breeze ruffles my hair. I run up the small hill until there it is—the river stretches out before me, huge and green and flowing. I run along the path and it's like me and the river, we move together. My breath steady, my strides long, I run stronger than ever before.

The water laps along the edges. Rocks glisten. Grass sways. Up ahead, I see my favorite spot, a bench under the shade of a big tree. I slow down to a jog, to a walk, and then I stop and sit.

Still holding tight to the envelope, I slip out a photo and letter. Baby May peeks out from a wide-brimmed sun hat, smiling a big, chubby-cheeked smile. I unfold the letter and read the last lines, like I've done over and over. *Her eyes are a beautiful brown, just like yours. We're thrilled that you will come and visit. On the back is a map to our home. Cell service is often spotty out here. Please plan on staying for supper.*

Today, finally, I'll see baby May again.

I'll hold her so gently. I'll run my finger along the soft skin of her tiny hand and count her dark eyelashes. I'll memorize the curve of her cheek and the soft wispy curls of her hair. Maybe I'll give her a bottle and feel how she sinks into the curve of my arm, and when she drifts off to sleep, I'll stay there, watching her breathe in and out and then I'll kiss her right on the tippy top of her head.

Carefully, I slide the letter and photo back into the envelope. I remember the photo wall in my bedroom; it's been over a year since I've added any. Not one single picture. But now, I know just how to start.

I relax back into the bench until I hear the thump of footsteps. Someone is walking over and, at first, with the sun shining down so bright, I can't tell who it is, but then, of course, I know that walk.

"How did you know I was here?" I ask, smiling big as the bridge.

"It's an important day. I figured you'd be here," says Lyde, as he hands me a white paper bag.

"What's this?"

"Open it."

I unfold the top. Inside are two pink-topped Mexican pastries. I laugh. "Ha! My favorite!" I take one out and hand him the other. "Seriously, you're the best." I take a delicious sugary bite. "I'm going to miss these." We sit there eating the pastries, a breeze stirring around us.

"You know, they probably won't have Mexican bakeries at Portland State University," he says.

I give him as shove. "No! They have to."

"But, I did find a great one in Seattle across the street from my dorm room."

"Promise to mail me some?" I ask.

"Nah, they'd go stale," he says.

"Then, I must come visit." I say. "It's an easy three-and-a-half hour train from Portland to Seattle."

"Or from Seattle to Portland," he says.

I smile and look out across the river, so wide and huge. It's not fast but it's moving.

"Are you worried about starting college?" asks Lyde.

I shake my head. Mom helped me apply for scholarships. I'm set for the first year, and as long as I keep my grades up, they will last through graduation. "I'm mostly worried about my mom and dad stalking me. They insist on moving me in and they already have a minute-by-minute plan of what we'll do on parents' weekend."

He laughs.

Something rustles and then I see them, two black-headed geese. They poke their heads up from the grass. They stare at Lyde and me and start honking like they're trying to tell us something. There's more rustling and they break through the thick grass and come waddling out onto the path. They look at each other, honk some more, and waddle faster. They flap into a run and then take off flying, soaring right along with the river.

Did you enjoy *Love, God, and Mexican Pastries*?

Please help this book reach more readers

by

leaving a review at

Amazon, Barnesandnoble, Goodreads

and/or any other book-loving sites.

Ready for more?

Please visit me at:

www.kfripley.com

Acknowledgments

I'D LIKE TO THANK:

My niece Karina who chose to place her baby for adoption. Karina's journey and her decision, though completely different from this fictional account, has, for years, filled me with awe. Her selflessness, love, and faith testify of her divineness and the glorious light in all of us.

My husband Brent, whose faith is greater than my own. This book simply wouldn't *be* without him, and I wouldn't be me without him. My kiddos: Sara, Amanda, Joshua, and Megan for their giant hearts, big brains, faith, creative gifts, and resilience. They inspire me and make me laugh every day. Now kids—are you wearing clean socks?

The Best Parents Ever, Carol and H.W. "Pete" Felsted. I love them dearly and can hear them cheering me on from heaven above. My supportive siblings: Scott, Ralene, Marc, Janell, Angela for much love, support, and giving me decades worth of writing material. Also, my extended family, several of whom inspire me with their own adoption stories: the Felsted, Leonardson, Klein, Ripley, and Rucker families.

My incredible friends, my Springville and Mapleton homies, who pick me up, dust me off, and set me right again. With an extra shout out to Amber Pickering, Ellie

Young, Judy Sumsion, Julie Stock, Kaylynn Hickman, Kevin Klein, Lisa Merrill, Mélissa Venet, Noelle Smith, Shannon Pexton, Tonya Gage, Valerie Savage, and Wendy LeFevre.

My writing buddies: JaNeal Freeman, Linda Bethers and Tessa Hauglid for their friendship, writing expertise, and encouragement, from the sloppy first drafts to… well, I hope they stay with me forever.

The perennials: Laura Byrne, Bonnie Berry LaMon, Sharon Van Zandt, Linda Washington for loving Melina, sending weekly and sometimes daily encouragement, and sharing their wisdom in draft after draft.

My brilliant and generous mentors from Vermont College of Fine Arts: Jane Kurtz, Julie Larios, Franny Billingsley, Uma Krishnaswami, and Amanda Jenkins. My classmates, the fabulous Secret Gardeners. The ever-gracious Martine Leavitt who mentored me, time after time, as I fan-stalked her through WIFYR, VCFA, and BYU.

The founders, faculty, staff, and participants of the WIFYR writing conference where my writing addiction started, especially Ann Cannon and Claudia Mills.

My editor, Kate Angelella, who worked miracles on this story. Her wisdom, enthusiasm, kindness, and sense of humor made the whole process joyful.

Finally, all birth parents, adoptive parents, or adoptees who may read this book. I pray it reads as a love letter. I have the deepest respect, love, and admiration for you.

About the Author

Karen Felsted Ripley (www.kfripley.com) is from Pasco, Washington. As a teen and young adult, she failed at love more times than she wants to remember. After years of getting it wrong, she finally hit the jackpot. Married with four children, she now lives in Utah and enjoys all things outdoorsy. She has an MFA in writing for children and young adults from Vermont College of Fine Arts. She also has an ongoing love affair with bakeries of all kinds, especially Mexican *Pastelerías*.

Made in the USA
San Bernardino, CA
10 January 2020

62978077R00171